A
Harlequin
Romance

OTHER
Harlequin Romances
by ELIZABETH ASHTON

Many of these titles are available at your local bookseller,
or through the Harlequin Reader Service.

For a free catalogue listing all available Harlequin Romances,
send your name and address to:

HARLEQUIN READER SERVICE,
M.P.O. Box 707, Niagara Falls, N.Y. 14302
Canadian address: Stratford, Ontario, Canada.

or use order coupon at back of book.

SIGH NO MORE

by

ELIZABETH ASHTON

HARLEQUIN BOOKS   TORONTO
WINNIPEG

Original hard cover edition published in 1973
by Mills & Boon Limited.

© Elizabeth Ashton 1973

SBN 373-01762-6

Harlequin edition published March 1974

The Harlequin trade mark, consisting of the word
HARLEQUIN and the portrayal of a Harlequin, is registered
in the United States Patent Office and in the Canada Trade
Marks Office.

Printed in Canada

Sigh no more, ladies,
Men were deceivers ever.

SHAKESPEARE: *Much Ado About Nothing*

CHAPTER ONE

'IT's snowing again,' Vivien said, as she drew back the curtains to disclose a tumble of white flakes falling out of a grey sky.

She was a tall girl, darkly beautiful, her scarlet wrapper giving a cheerful note to the cold, dull morning. Her companion, lying on the divan before the gas fire, thought for the hundredth time how lovely she was, with her night-black hair and huge dark eyes.

Vivien turned from the window and looked at the other girl compassionately.

'How do you feel this morning?'

'I'm heaps better.' She moved aside the breakfast tray from her knees. 'You shouldn't cosset me, Viv, there's nothing really wrong with me now, except for being in quarantine.'

Imogen Sinclair was recovering from an ill-timed attack of measles, which she had neglected to have when she was a child, an indisposition which had been particularly unfortunate, as she had just secured a much-coveted engagement on television. She was a dancer by profession, and though she had not rated ballet, she had been lucky enough to obtain work in various musical shows, since she had left her training school.

Vivien shrugged her shoulders and lit a cigarette. She too was in the profession, and was playing a small part in a West End play.

'Since I'm at home most mornings, you might as well take advantage of my ministrations,' she said lightly. 'You still look far from well.'

Her eyes lingered upon the younger girl with genuine affection. Imogen's looks were much less spectacular than her friend's. She was not so tall, with a heart-shaped piquant face. Her colouring was unusual—dark auburn hair, black in shadow, red-lit in sunlight, creamy skin and greenish eyes under ebony, winged brows, which tilted upwards at the outer corners. Her great attraction was her vitality and verve, but those her illness had quenched. She was pale and listless, but Vivien knew that her languor was less due to the measles than a troubled spirit.

The two girls shared a flat with a third, Louise Lambert, whose trade was secretarial and much less glamorous than her mates'. They rented a top-floor flat in the wilderness of old Victorian property between Kilburn and Hampstead, and thought themselves fortunate to find a place so central at a rent which was within their means. There were only two rooms, a kitchenette and a bathroom, and space was cramped. Vivien and Louise shared the small bedroom, but Imogen slept on the convertible divan in the living-room, where she was now reposing.

'Were there any letters?' she asked eagerly.

'Three, and all for you.' Vivien drew the envelopes from the pocket of her gown. She had withheld them until Imogen had eaten her breakfast, for she had guessed the author of one of them from the boldly scrawled inscription, and knowing what she knew, feared its contents would take away what there was of her friend's small appetite.

Imogen seized upon it, crying, 'Ray, at last!'

'About time too,' Vivien commented. She picked up the tray and carried it into the kitchenette, closing the door behind her.

With trembling fingers, Imogen tore open the green envelope with its multi-coloured lining. Raymond Benito, the last being a stage name, affected exotic stationery when he could bring himself to put pen to paper, a

8

fact Imogen noted with a little tender smile.

She knew him so well, for they had been friends ever since their childhood, when she had striven to take part in his boyish sports. He had always tried to include her, though his friends had jeered, but he had pointed out that she was useful for retrieving balls, and minding their coats when they played impromptu football, and they had come to accept her presence, while she fetched and carried and adored the handsome Raymond. The great bond between them was their love of dancing. From their earliest years, both had insisted that they wanted to make the art their career. Their respective parents had raised no obstacles and both had trained together, afterwards seeking joint engagements. They had appeared together in the choruses of pantomimes, revues, musicals and ice shows, bound by a mutual promise that neither would accept an engagement without the other. They had both been elated when they had obtained the job on television, dancing in a chorus of youngsters supporting a singing star. Unfortunately the series was transmitted live, and Imogen's illness meant that she had to be replaced.

Ray, she knew, hated sickness and was terrified of infection. She had not expected him to come and see her, even though he had had the complaint, for though the chances of contracting a second dose were remote, it was possible.

He had sent her flowers when he heard about her indisposition, but since then she had heard nothing; he had neither rung up nor written. Vivien, at her request, had tried to contact him over the telephone, but without success; he was always out.

Vivien had looked at her strangely, when she had said:

'He'll think no more of you for running after him. No doubt you'll hear from him in time. Bit of a fair-weather friend, isn't he?'

'You always think the worst of everything male,' Imogen had retorted. 'I expect he's very busy.' But she had been hurt by his neglect, for Raymond was much more than a friend. Confidently she expected that their professional partnership would eventually become a matrimonial one. She loved him, and he had said he loved her. She had never looked at another boy, though plenty had looked at her.

She opened the sprawled sheets and began to read them avidly. She had had letters from Ray before, upon the rare occasions when they had been parted for a few days, passionate effusions, which she treasured, never doubting that they were genuine, and not what he thought she wanted to hear.

To her disappointment this one was almost perfunctory.

He started with a few jocular enquiries about her spots, refusing to recognise that she had been seriously ill, so much so that the doctor had suggested moving her into hospital. Vivien, who knew how she loathed hospitals, had stoutly maintained that they could manage with the help of the local nurse, since she was home for a large part of the day, and Louise was there at night, when she went to the theatre. Between them, her two devoted friends had pulled her through.

Raymond's letter went on to tell her that he had obtained an engagement in a musical show under the auspices of a woman called Janice Webster, now the television series was ending, and he would be touring in Australia for six to eight weeks. He was sorry he could not wait for her recovery, but in their chancy profession, a man had to take what came along. He had already started rehearsing and was rushed off his feet, and since she was still in purdah, as he put it, it would be impossible to come and say goodbye.

Imogen let the bright green sheet drop with a constricted feeling about her heart. Her quarantine was nearly over; in any case, the risk was now very slight. She knew perfectly well that Raymond was using it as an excuse not to see her. He was going away for nearly two months, and the conviction grew upon her that this was the end.

She stared at the square of window outside which the snowflakes still fell. Even so, the day was less bleak than the prospect before her.

Vivien came back into the room, and one look at Imogen's face told her that the blow had fallen. She had been expecting it. In the dressing-rooms at the theatre, she heard all the theatrical gossip. Janice Webster and her young male dancers were a scandalous joke, and Raymond Benito had been her latest acquisition.

Vivien had never approved of him, sensing that beneath his good looks and surface charm he was a fickle and irresponsible creature. In her opinion, Imogen was wasting herself upon him, he would inevitably let her down sooner or later, but she was too wise to criticise him to her friend, for she also knew that love is blind.

Even now, she held her peace, but stood waiting for Imogen to speak.

'He's going away,' Imogen said blankly. 'It'll be the first time we've ever been parted since I've known him, and . . . Oh, Viv, I don't think he'll come back.'

Vivien sat down on the divan beside her, determined not to raise false hopes.

'I'm sorry, Imo,' she said gently. 'I've seen this coming. He's no good, my pet, and that Janice woman has got him in tow. She's a bloodsucker where young men are concerned.'

'But, Viv, how can he? She's years older than he is.'

'Boys are often attracted by mature women,' Vivien pointed out, adding vindictively, 'I hope she gives him hell, and she probably will too.'

Being still weak, Imogen began to cry despairingly.

'I want to die,' she sobbed.

'Rubbish!' Vivien exclaimed vigorously. 'Die for that drip? You've all your life before you, my pet, you're only nineteen. You'll get over Ray, he never was good enough for you, and you're attractive, Imo, men like you. You'll be able to pick a better one than Ray, though they're all tarred with the same brush. Still, you couldn't have made a worse choice.'

'He was good enough for me.' Imogen scrubbed her eyes with her handkerchief. 'I've never wanted anyone else.'

'More fool you.' Vivien leaned back against the wall and fumbled for her cigarettes. She was an inveterate smoker. 'I thought the sun had fallen out of the sky when Bill and I broke up, but I didn't commit suicide nor become a nun. As you know, we, like you and Ray, were childhood sweethearts. Like an idiot I insisted upon marrying him when I was sixteen, and though our parents demurred they didn't oppose us. Talk about being wet behind the ears! I was all starry-eyed bliss and imagined love lasted for ever.'

She lit her cigarette and blew out a cloud of smoke.

'Of course we were both much too young and soon found out our mistake. But if I didn't know my way about then, I do now. Men can be brutes, but they can also be fun. I swore when we were divorced, that I'd never allow myself to become emotionally involved with a man again, and I've kept my oath. If they do, it's just too bad for them, I soon tell them where they get off. I look upon men as free meal tickets and necessary dancing partners and when the break comes, it isn't me who gets ditched.'

Having expounded her philosophy, Vivien got up and went in search of an ashtray, while Imogen looked at her curiously. She was such a lovely creature and she had been so kind to herself, but towards the opposite sex she was as hard as granite.

She had always been a little shocked by Vivien's mercenary attitude towards her many admirers, but knowing that her marriage had failed, she had made allowances for her. Now, in the midst of her own heartbreak, she found her friend's cynicism consoling. But she knew that for all her bravado, Vivien was not happy, which suggested her heartless attitude was not altogether satisfactory.

She knew that she could never bring herself to exploit her own boy-friends as her friend did hers, even to assuage her wounded vanity, but she also knew that Vivien was motivated more by a desire for revenge than vanity. There was a certain amount of sense in her outbreak, for if Raymond, in whose love and fidelity Imogen had had implicit faith, had deserted her, how could she ever believe in another man's protestations?

'You don't believe in love, do you, Viv?' she asked tentatively.

'I do not. Sentimental moonshine! Bill and I thought we loved, and we ended up like cat and dog. Falling in love is a snare and delusion. It doesn't last beyond the first fine careless rapture. You wake up one morning and find the man you believed was so wonderful is just an ordinary guy with a lot of irritating habits and shortcomings and he's thinking the same of you. If you're lucky, you may manage to adjust after a lot of ups and downs, but I wasn't lucky. You've had an escape, my love, for Ray would have made a shocking husband, though I've never dared to point it out before, you were so besotted.'

'He ... he had his points,' Imogen said weakly, trying to defend her faithless swain.

'None that I could see. He wouldn't have even been a good provider, and if ever I'm crazy enough to marry again, that's what I shall look for. Luxuries can compensate for a lot of heartache. But don't you be in any hurry, marriage isn't all it's cracked up to be. Look around and enjoy your fun, and if a man shows signs of becoming serious, show him the door.' She laughed bitterly. 'What they call love has a much less pretty name.'

Vivien attracted men as a jampot does wasps. She was seldom without a cavalier, but never the same one for long. Imogen admired her cool assurance and sophistication. Vaguely she wondered if she could ever emulate it. She was quite sure her emotions would never be aroused by any future contacts. Her heart was dead for ever, but male admiration could always give a woman a kick. Not that at that moment she had any desire for men friends of any description, all she wanted was a refuge where she could creep away and lick her wounds.

'You had two other letters,' Vivien reminded her.

Imogen opened them without much interest. One was the usual weekly screed from her mother. The Sinclairs were an unworldly elderly couple, who had married late in life, and Imogen was their only child. Her father was a clergyman and both he and his wife were deeply immersed in parochial affairs. He had been ill, the result of the wintry weather, and Mrs Sinclair bewailed the fact that she had been unable because of that to come to town to visit her daughter. If Imogen were sufficiently recovered, she must come home to recuperate. The invitation was not very warm; reading between the lines, Imogen suspected that her mother did not feel equal to coping with two invalids, but as she was no longer ill, she would be expected to help wait upon her father. Fond though she was of her parents, she did not feel quite equal to such service, and the big old vicarage would be very dreary and draughty at that time of the year. Moreover, the village would be full of memories of Raymond, for he had been the boy next door.

Then she noticed there was a scrawled postscript. Lettice Wainwright had been on the phone and had suggested that Imogen might alternatively like to go to visit her in Derbyshire.

'If she writes and confirms her invitation, go,' Mrs Sinclair had written, 'it would be such a nice change for you.'

The third letter was the invitation from Lettice. The Wainwrights were old friends of the Sinclairs. Before moving up north they had lived in the same village. Lettice was a lively young woman, whom the teenage Imogen had liked. She had been sorry when they had moved away with their little boy and baby daughter.

'I know it's not the ideal time to come up to Derbyshire,' Lettice wrote, 'but as your mother has her hands full with your father, it seems a solution for you. We'd love to have you, and at least our house is warm, not like your impossible great vicarage. I know you're fond of children and my two are at a delightful age now. Perhaps they can keep you from feeling bored.'

'That sounds the very thing for you,' Vivien declared when Imogen had disclosed the contents of her correspondence. 'Much better than going home where, if you'll forgive me saying so, your mother will only unload her own woes upon you. You need cheerful society and children can be balm to heartache. You like these Wainwrights?'

'Very much. Joe is a lot older than Letty, but he's nice. She's his second wife, and she used to be fun.'

'Then, honey, you go,' Vivien urged her. 'It's a nice long way away and won't hold any associations for you like your village does, and since your mother is agreeable, why not?'

There was nothing against the project except that Imogen felt lethargic, listless and disinclined to make any effort. Also she was cherishing a faint hope that Raymond might at the last moment decide to come and see her. She still could not believe that he had really given her up. Vivien knew perfectly well why her friend still lingered in London, and sighed over her folly.

Then a chance encounter with the young man himself enabled her to convince her friend of the futility of waiting. She did not mean to be unkind, but she was certain that the sooner Imogen made a clean break with her past, the better it would be for her.

She had run into Raymond on the platform of a tube station while they were both waiting for a train, and though he had tried not to see her, she had gone up to him and told him bluntly what she thought of his conduct.

He had laughed at her and said:

'No need to blow your top, beautiful, you can't revive dead ashes. I was fond enough of Imo when we were younger, but we're grown up now, or at least I am; she's still rather juvenile. All she feels for me is a schoolgirl's crush and she'll soon get over it. The truth is I need someone more mature.'

He was only two years older than Imogen.

'Gone to the other extreme, haven't you?' Vivien had snapped. 'Janice Webster's no chicken.'

'Who said anything about her?' he had asked, but he had looked guilty.

The train came in with a woosh, and he added hurriedly:

' 'Bye, Viv, you won't be seeing me for a while—and impress upon Imo that it's finished.'

The gist of this conversation Vivien passed on to Imogen in a softened version.

'Go up to Derbyshire and forget him,' she urged.

But it was not easy to forget an association which had lasted so many years.

Louise unconsciously provided a further irritant which succeeded in driving Imogen out of the flat. She had for some time been going steady with a clerk at the office where she worked. Now she announced that she was at last engaged, and her Godfrey was continually in and out of the flatlet. Louise was plain, plump and singularly tactless. Her fiancé matched her, being small, sandy and insignificant. Vivien said a little maliciously to Imogen in private:

'Neither you nor I would look at him, but I expect he was the best she could get.'

Louise seemed highly satisfied with her conquest. She went around starry-eyed, displaying her ring to all comers. Imogen found her rhapsodies trying, especially when with her usual obtuseness she compared her luck with having her man present while Imogen's was far away, for Imogen had not confided in her, merely saying Raymond was on tour.

'That's the worst of theatrical life,' Louise said smugly, 'you're always being separated. No wonder the divorce rate is so high in the profession. Now Godfrey's in a steady job and he'll never have to go away without me.'

She was secretly a little jealous of her friends' more glamorous occupations, but she was a good-hearted girl, and would have been sympathetic if she had known the real situation between Raymond and Imogen, but the latter could not face the commiseration which she knew would be all too volubly expressed if she put her wise.

This engagement was the spur Imogen needed to send her north, and she accepted Lettice Wainwright's invitation without further hesitation.

There was no change in the weather when Imogen left London. It was still snowing. It had been an exceptionally severe winter. From Christmas onwards it had snowed, and now in mid-February the country still huddled in the grip of frost under its white mantle. As always, the arctic weather had taken Britain by surprise. Pipes froze, roads became impassable and the electricity supply was strained to its limit.

The long-distance train was fortunately for her adequately heated, but the branch-line connection was not so good. Imogen regretted the change as she huddled into her coat in a window seat, while she looked out at the grey February dusk. The landscape lay feet deep in snow and the leaden sky promised more to come. It looked exceedingly dreary and she wondered why on earth she had left the bright lights of London to come into this frozen wilderness.

With a hoot, the train entered a tunnel through the hills, and turning away from the blacked-out window, she met the eyes of a young man sitting opposite to her. She had been aware of his interest ever since they had left the junction, but had purposely avoided his glance. She had no wish to strike up an acquaintanceship with him, and this last leg of her journey was a short one.

She noticed that he was little more than a boy, with dark eyes set in a thin, eager face, while above his brow his dark hair waved attractively. Something about him, the set of his head, his thin, nervous body, the way his hair grew, reminded her of Raymond, and he was the last person she wanted to have recalled to her.

Under Vivien's tutelage she had resolved that any future advances from young men were to be met with cool detachment, but since her illness, she had looked so pale and drawn, she thought it was unlikely that she would receive any. But it seemed she was wrong, for here was a youth, with a look of Raymond, making sheep's eyes at her across the width of the railway compartment. She was unaware that her delicate appearance gave her a kind of wistful fragility, which appealed to a protective streak in her companion. What she was aware of was that the faint resemblance to Raymond was pulling at her heart-strings—the heart which she was determined should be impervious to emotion. It was most disconcerting to realise that she was still vulnerable. But it was only the look of Ray that had moved her, she told herself, as she hastily turned her attention back to the window, and hoped the train would soon reach her stop.

To her surprise, the young man leaned forward and asked:

'Are you by any chance the Miss Sinclair from London, who is coming to stay with the Wainwrights?'

Wondering who he could be, she admitted that she was.

'I live next door,' he went on, as the train left the tunnel and drew up at a small station. 'No, this isn't it, ours is the next stop,' as she peered out to read the station's name. She saw in the faint light that they were in a deep valley with snow-clad slopes rising up on either side, which she found depressing.

'Lettice told me to look out for you so that I could give you a lift up from the station,' her companion went on. 'My name's Peter Lethwaite.' He held out a thin brown hand and reluctantly she laid hers in it.

'It stays very cold,' she said for the sake of something to say.

'Yes, we've had exceptional snow this year. Fine for winter sports,' he sounded pleased. 'We can even ski down those slopes,' he indicated the chill scene outside. 'Have you ever skied?'

'No, but I can skate.'

One Christmas she had been in an ice show with Raymond; why did everything have to remind her of him?

'There's been some of that on the reservoir,' he told her.

The train continued its way, passing between high

hills upon which the night was descending out of a darkening sky.

'By the look of it it's going to snow some more,' Peter said gleefully, while Imogen shivered, thinking snowfalls could mean different things to different people. She did not like the stuff except on a Christmas card.

The train ran into the station and Imogen stood up to reach her suitcase from the rack, but Peter forestalled her.

'Is this all, or is there more in the van?'

'No. Only these two cases.' She had a smaller one beside her. 'I don't expect I'll be staying long.'

'Oh, what a pity.' Regret sounded in his voice. 'From what Letty said, I thought it would be quite a while.'

He opened the door for her, and followed her on to the platform carrying her two cases.

'My car's outside,' he told her. 'It's a little way up to Castleton, too far for you to walk. You see, I work in Chinley, but I got off early today to meet you.'

The car, a Mini, was outside the station with a blanket thrown over its bonnet.

'I hope she'll start,' he said anxiously, as he piled her luggage on to the back seat. Meanwhile Imogen looked around her. The valley here was more open and the hills were veiled by the night. Only the snow glimmered palely on either side of them.

The Mini did start over a road that had been ploughed and salted. They turned off over a river and began to climb.

'Do you know this part of the world?' Peter asked.

'No, my home is in Hertfordshire. I haven't stayed with the Wainwrights since they moved north.'

'So Letty said. You'll like it here, I'm sure.'

Imogen said nothing. She doubted it.

Castleton crouched at the foot of the hills, a little grey town overlooked by its ruined castle, but she could see nothing of it that evening except for the vague shapes of houses and the piles of dirty snow scraped off the road, illuminated feebly by scattered street lights.

Peter drew up in front of a low stone house, from which lights were pouring from the uncurtained windows.

'Here we are. Barley Howe, and all lit up in your honour.'

Imogen climbed out of the restricted space of the little car, realising she was cold and stiff. She had been travelling for most of the day. She walked carefully up the short flagged path to the front door, which had been cleared of snow, but had iced over, and was slippery. Peter followed carrying her cases.

The inmates of the house must have heard the car arrive, for the front door opened before she reached it, and Lettice Wainwright stood on the threshold with her two small children peering round her trousered legs.

Lettice was small, thin and impulsive. She embraced the taller girl enthusiastically, and drew her inside the house.

'My dear, you must be frozen!' she exclaimed. 'Such weather! And they say the cold spell is going on.' The last two words were uttered with almost tragic emphasis. 'Come and get warm before you go upstairs ... Pete...' calling over her shoulder, 'take Imogen's cases upstairs, please, it's the blue room.'

She led Imogen into the sitting-room followed by the two children. It was a long low-ceilinged room with a lived in look. The furniture was worn but comfortable. A huge coal fire blazed on the hearth. Lettice steered Imogen towards a big armchair set before it. From the opposite side of the hearth, her host, Joseph Wainwright, rose to greet her.

She had known him for most of her life, for he had

been resident in her Hertfordshire village before his second marriage. 'Handsome Joe', he had been called, and had been the object of much speculation among the village spinsters. It was known that his wife, a Swedish girl, had left him to return to her own country, taking her two children with her. Once a year they came to visit him.

He had a housekeeper to look after him, but whether he were divorced and eligible was the burning question. Apparently he was, for after a protracted stay away he had returned, bringing a young bride with him, much to the disgust of the unmarried women, who felt they had been slighted. Lettice, they said, was a flighty piece and much too young for him, but there was no fool like an old fool.

However, to their chagrin, the couple seemed happy. Lettice produced two babies and eventually they moved north.

Joe had retained his good looks, though his face had become lined and there were silver streaks in his hair. He was a big, quiet man and the hand which enfolded Imogen's gripped firmly, while he uttered a friendly greeting.

The children regarded the visitor solemnly. Teddy was six, a sturdy handsome child, his sister Pamela was four, with flying blonde hair and bright blue eyes. She looked like a cherub but was an imp.

'Have you brought us anything?' Teddy demanded.

Both parents turned and rent him. That was not what one asked a guest upon arrival. Lettice apologised. Children were so spoiled nowadays. They were given so much and expected more. Imogen, who had in fact brought a small gift for each of them, decided it was not the right moment to produce them.

In the lull that followed, Pam said in a loud voice:

'Yes, but *has* she?'

Lettice threw up her hands. 'I give up!'

Imogen said diplomatically: 'Wait and see.'

'How long must me wait and see?' Pam demanded, who still got her pronouns mixed. 'Until after tea?'

'Certainly until after tea,' her mother told her. 'Oh, there you are, Pete,' as the young man came in. 'You'll stay and have a cup of tea?'

Peter's eyes had gone straight to Imogen. She had opened her travelling coat, beneath which she wore a green wool dress. The firelight flickered on her hair, picking out the ruddy lights amid its darkness. Her short skirt revealed her knees and slender legs terminating in fine ankles and narrow feet. He hesitated.

'Really I ought to go home. Mother'll have tea ready for me.'

'Just stay for a cuppa,' Letty urged kindly, noticing the direction of his gaze with amusement. 'It's all ready.'

Peter pulled up a tuffet and sat down on it at Imogen's feet with a sigh of content.

A substantial meal was brought in on a wheeled trolley.

'We only have a light supper,' Lettice explained, 'and I don't suppose you had much to eat on the train.'

Imogen admitted to a few sandwiches and coffee in the buffet car. She had fallen in with her hosts' suggestion that she should stay where she was until she was 'de-iced'. She slipped off her coat and Peter sprang up to assist her, carrying it away to hang in the hall. Evidently he was at home at Barley Howe. She wished he was not. Plainly he was attracted by her, but he was too young, too boyish to be the right material to exploit if she were going to follow Vivien's advice. But Raymond too had been only a boy when she first knew him, and his early infatuation had not lasted. Neither would Peter's, she felt sure, if she were weak enough to take him seriously.

She relaxed in the warmth of the room and her

hosts' pleasant company. The children were placed at a distance at a small table. Peter brought her a cup of tea and a stool to put it upon. She ate toasted scones, sandwiches and home-baked cake—Letty did most of her own cooking—while they asked her about her family, her illness and her life in London.

'I don't altogether approve of girls living on their own,' Letty commented, when Imogen had described her flat and friends. 'They don't eat enough.' She looked critically at Imogen's slight figure which looked lost in the big chair.

'I mustn't get fat, I'm a dancer,' Imogen pointed out.

'We saw you in your television show,' Lettice told her, 'too bad you couldn't finish it.'

Imogen felt a stab. She had been so happy in that show, with no inkling of what was about to happen—but her friends did not know about Raymond, and she had no intention of telling them.

Their tea despatched, the children demanded television, which was allowed, so long as they kept it low.

'For we want to talk,' Lettice told them, and Joe added, 'Television's anti-social.'

The telephone rang in the hall and Lettice flew to answer it, while Joe commented that it was probably for him, but his wife was so restless she could not keep still.

Imogen looked at him speculatively. Outwardly he was a devoted husband, but what secrets did that handsome face conceal? It was so easy for men, whose work took them out of the house, to lead a double life. Since her own bitter experience, she would always wonder and be suspicious, and Joseph's first wife had deserted him, ostensibly because she pined for her own country, but there might have been other reasons.

'Penny for them,' Peter said.

'Not worth even a new penny,' she told him, smiling.

24

'In fact I'm half asleep. It's the hot fire and the good tea.'

Lettice stuck her head round the door.

'Do you know if Erica Brayshaw's at home?' she asked.

'Gone to Buxton for the weekend,' Peter called back.

'Oh dear, Christian will be put out.' She vanished.

'Christian?' Peter exclaimed, jumping to his feet. 'It must be him on the phone. I didn't know he was back.'

'The games finished last week,' Joseph reminded him. He turned to Imogen. 'We're very proud of my son Christian. He's won a gold medal for skiing. Did you ever meet him?'

'No. I always seemed to miss his visits when he came to Hertfordshire.'

Christian and his twin sister Greta had lived with their mother while she was still alive, and their annual visit to their father had never seemed to coincide with her own holidays. They were, she knew, somewhat older than herself.

Lettice came back with a transfigured face, joy shone in her eyes and radiated from her smiling lips.

'Christian is coming to see us, he'll be arriving late tonight. Isn't it wonderful?' She obviously adored her stepson.

Teddy tore himself away from the thrills of television to cry excitedly. 'Chris coming? He's sure to bring us something super,' with a baleful glance at Imogen.

'Mercenary brat!' reproved his father. 'How come Christian is honouring us with a visit in the skiing season, Letty? He's usually tied up with competitions.'

For Christian Wainwright had inherited private means from his mother and was able to devote himself entirely to that sport. Having spent his childhood in Sweden, where youngsters can ski and skate almost as soon as they can walk, he had developed a passion for skiing, and it had become his main interest in life.

'It's something to do with Greta,' Lettice said vaguely. 'He said he'd explain when he came.'

Joseph looked concerned. Since her marriage and recent widowhood, he had almost lost touch with his elder daughter.

'I hope nothing's wrong,' he said.

Peter, to whom Greta was only a name as she was to Imogen, muttered perfunctorily that he hoped not, then added enthusiasically that with the unprecedented snowfalls there was skiing up on Rushup Edge and Christian could indulge his favourite pastime.

'Perhaps that's why he's coming,' he suggested.

'Hardly that,' Joseph laughed. 'After the pistes in Switzerland and Austria our little hills will be very small beer to him. However, I don't doubt he'll go out with you, if that's what you're hoping,' and added to Imogen, 'My elder son is dedicated to a life on skis. He's won several of the big races.'

Pride sounded in his voice and shone in his eyes.

'I've spent winter sports holidays where he was competing,' Peter supplemented, with the reverence of hero-worship. 'He's marvellous!'

Imogen supposed that she would be expected to be impressed by such an athlete. Actually she felt a little scornful. She did not care for sporting types; they were usually completely absorbed by their chosen occupation and a dead loss socially.

'I'm afraid I know nothing about skiing,' she said.

'The deficiencies in your education will soon be made up,' Joseph told her, grinning, and she sighed. The prospect did not appeal to her. Feeling they would like to discuss Christian and Greta without her alien presence, she stood up and asked if she could go to her room and unpack.

'See you tomorrow,' Peter called after her, as Lettice

escorted her to the stairs.

Her room was low-ceilinged with a big, modern window inserted where the former small mullioned one had been. The furniture was a mixture of ancient and modern, with bright curtains and coverlet. An electric stove did its best to dispel the chill. After the confines of the flat it looked spacious.

'I hope you'll be comfortable here,' Lettice said. 'The bathroom's next door. Brr, I'll be glad when the thaw comes!'

'But wouldn't that disappoint your stepson?' Imogen asked.

'I don't suppose he'll stay long,' Lettice said a little sadly. 'Officially Barley Howe is his home, Joe asked him to consider it so when his mother died, but he's hardly ever here. I hope there's nothing wrong with Greta. She never comes to England now, though I did meet her in Stockholm. She's got two little children, and her husband's death would have been a tragedy if they'd got on, but I don't think they did. She's always been a bit antagonistic to me.'

'I imagine step-relationships aren't very easy,' Imogen suggested tactfully.

'But I get on splendidly with Christian. Of course he's a man, which I suppose makes a difference. He's most attractive, Imogen, all the girls are crazy about him, though he shows no signs of wanting to get married. Greta is quite different, she's much more Swedish than he is, and the Swedes are not a matey people, very cold and formal. Now if you'll forgive me, I must run away. I've got to get the kids to bed and see about his room. Come down when you're ready. Joe'll be there.'

Imogen slowly unpacked her belongings, which were mainly trousers and sweaters. She wished the latter had been thicker. Then she drew the heavy blue curtains and looked outside. There was nothing to be seen as the sky was overcast, only the white shimmer of the snow beneath her. Yet all around her were hills, she could sense them, though she could not see them. She was not sure that she liked hills, she preferred the gentle undulating countryside of the Midlands; it was less wild.

She wondered when Christian was expected, and wished that she had asked. If it was late she could go to bed early and avoid him. She had an inexplicable feeling that he was going to prove a disruptive element to the peace of her holiday. But perhaps he would only stay for the weekend, and apparently his interest was occupied elsewhere with the girl, Erica.

As it happened, she had her wish. Tired with her journey, Lettice packed her off to bed before his late arrival with a glass of hot milk.

But she heard him come—Lettice's cry of joyful welcome, the murmur of male voices in the hall—his was deeper than his father's—and his laughter, a gay sound with a hint of recklessness in it. She could picture the man, big, blond and conceited, for he must be conceited with so much adulation, the type of man who thought he was God's gift to women, and lapped up their admiration, even while he affected to despise it.

He had asked for a girl as soon as he had announced his coming. Erica—an unusual name; what was she? His fan, his flirt, perhaps even his mistress? Poor girl, she would be sick at having missed him. Hard luck for her!

But if Erica Brayshaw was absent, Imogen Sinclair was on the spot, an unexpected bonus, only she had no use for men, especially blond Nordic skiers, and that, if he made any advances, she would soon let him know. A little tingle of excitement ran up her spine. Peter Lethwaite would have to be handled with kid gloves, but Christian might present a challenge.

She fell asleep almost as soon as her head touched the pillow, without realising that absorbed in her speculations about the newcomer she had not once thought of Raymond.

CHAPTER TWO

IMOGEN awoke before the sun had risen, but her room was light from the reflected snow. Lettice had warned her that as it was Saturday breakfast would be leisurely and late. She sprang out of bed and swept back the curtains. There had been more snow in the night and then frost. The eastern sky was flushed with yellow light, precursor of the sun. Her window looked across the garden to the houses opposite, grey-stone buildings with slate roofs, but above them were the hills, steep slopes of virginal white thrusting upward into a clear sky.

Hastily she sought the bathroom, hoping to perform her abulutions before the family needed it. Those done, she dressed in slacks and an emerald green sweater that brought out the green in her eyes. Make-up, she decided, was unsuitable in such rural surroundings, nor did she need much, for nature had blessed her with dark brows and dark eyelashes.

The splodge of a snowball against her window pane caused her to look out. The sun was rising, its rays throwing golden shafts into the blue sky and causing the snow to sparkle.

Below her in the garden two young men were standing. One was Peter; the other, she surmised, was Christian, and she looked at him with frank interest, wondering how far he fell short of the mental picture she had drawn of him. In so far as he was tall and blond she had been correct, and the slightly arrogant carriage of his head might indicate that he had a good opinion of himself. Broad-shouldered and narrow-hipped, he was tanned by exposure to weather; bare-headed, his fair hair was gilded by the rising sun. The blue eyes raised to her window were keen and penetrating, the high bridged nose was slightly aquiline, the mouth too thin-lipped and satirical for beauty. He was vibrant with life and energy, and except that he was clean-shaven, might have modelled for one of his Viking ancestors. Even at this first glimpse of him, Imogen sensed he could be dangerously attractive.

But he'll cut no ice with me, she thought disdainfully, he's too obviously a heart-throb. Erica can keep him!

Peter mouthed something, and she threw up the sash to hear him. A blast of icy air swept into the room.

'Come out,' Peter called, 'but put a coat on. It's nippy, but it's glorious.'

Shivering, she pointed out that she had not breakfasted.

Christian looked at his watch. 'It won't be ready for a few minutes. Come out and get a freshener.'

Fresh, she thought was the operative word, as she closed the window. Wanting to see what Castleton looked like, she snatched up her coat and ran downstairs out into the diminutive garden.

Christian looked her up and down appraisingly.

'I was disappointed you didn't stop up to welcome me,' he told her. There was a disconcerting glint in his blue eyes.

'I'm sorry,' she said demurely, 'but surely you had a big enough welcoming committee without me? I was tired after my journey.'

'Of course she was,' Peter chimed in. 'Don't be so vain, Christian. Why should she wait up to see you?'

'Why indeed, except she might have been curious to see what I'd grown up into.'

'But I've never seen you before,' she said, surprised.

'Oh yes, you have. You were an adorable monkey with a thatch of black hair, about eighteen months

31

old, I should say—I know you weren't very steady on your pins. Unfortunately when I picked you up, you were sick all over my new pullover. That was what made it one of my boyhood's memorable occasions. Your mother, while she mopped me up, explained that it was too soon after dinner for gymnastics.'

'Meaning you did rather more than pick her up?' Peter said, looking as if he envied Christian his earlier opportunities.

'Well, I swung her about a bit, and she enjoyed it—laughed her head off, until she was sick.'

'Naturally I can't remember anything about it,' Imogen said with hauteur. 'That is, if it ever happened, which I doubt.'

She suspected he was embroidering this early encounter in revenge for her neglect of the night before.

'Oh, it happened. Why should I make it up? You haven't changed. You still look adorable and are, I suspect, an imp.'

'Oh really!' She was annoyed by this blatant approach. 'You don't have to.'

'Have to what?'

'Lay it on with a trowel. I prefer sincerity to compliments.'

'It wasn't entirely complimentary,' he returned, 'or do you like being called an imp? You haven't grown a great deal, Imogen, I could pick you up with ease, though I hope you can now control your nausea.'

'You're being quite absurd!' she said loftily, then, arrested by the scene before her, exclaimed, 'How lovely!'

They had passed beyond the houses, and looking back she could see the whole range of hills behind the town, rising to her right above the crags of the Winnats Pass to the moors beyond, and, as she slowly turned, continued past the conical summit of Mam Tor to a further range of undulating heights on the

32

far side of the Hope Valley.

'Yes, it is, isn't it?' Peter said eagerly, who had been becoming increasingly restive during her exchange with Christian. 'Look, you can see the Castle above that mass of trees. It's only a ruin, but there's a lot of the curtain wall still standing. It must have been impregnable, because there's a steep drop to Cave Dale on the other side, and on this side, the keep is above a sheer fall of rock to Peak Cavern below it. I must take you up and show you round.'

'When I've gone,' Christian said firmly, 'or the snow has. Today we have other things to do. As soon as we've had breakfast, we'll try Rushup Edge for skiing.'

Good, that will get them both out of the way, Imogen thought with satisfaction. She had discovered that there was something disturbing in Christian's proximity, and though she was excited by it, she would prefer to be left to her own devices.

That was not to be.

They returned to the house, and Peter left them to go next door, promising to return as soon as he had had his meal.

The children were delighted by the bright day.

'You'll take our toboggan up to the top of the hill, won't you, Chris?' Teddy asked coaxingly.

'Yes, please, please!' Pamela cried.

He smiled affectionately at his half-brother and sister. 'Why, sure, it'll go in my car. Letty, still got your skis?'

'They're somewhere around,' she said vaguely, 'but you're not going to get me on to them today. Perhaps Imogen would like to have a go. I think she takes the same size as I do, so she can borrow my boots.'

Imogen hastily disclaimed any desire to ski, while Christian looked at her doubtfully.

'But you should be good at it,' Lettice persisted. 'With all your dancing training you should have good balance, and you can skate.'

'Is that so?' Christian drawled, and Imogen realised that he doubted her ability. Instantly she decided she would show him she was not the hothouse plant he seemed to imagine.

'I'd like to have a shot at it,' she declared.

'Good,' Joseph approved her spirit. 'And since Christian aspires to become an instructor eventually, teaching you will give him some practice.'

Imogen looked at Christian provocatively. 'If it isn't troubling you too much,' she said sweetly.

He grinned. 'I shall put you through it,' he warned.

'I'm not scared. I've been through the mill before, and I don't suppose you could do an entrechat.'

'Nor you a christiana,' he returned. 'We're going to have a busy morning.'

There was an edge to his tone which made her wonder what she was letting herself in for, but if he thought she was going to let him bully her, he would discover his mistake.

Lettice's ski clothes fitted her perfectly. Lettice had learned to ski when she had accompanied her husband on winter sports holidays in Europe, but she was not very keen.

Feeling a little self-conscious in her borrowed plumes, Imogen joined the excited children while they waited for Christian to bring his car round. This being an estate convertible had ample room, not only for the family but also their gear, including the toboggan and skis. Peter joined them, and raised his brows when he saw Imogen's outfit.

'So you do ski?'

'Not yet. Christian is going to teach me.'

'Oh.' He looked blank.

Christian drove them up the winding road that went past the base of Mam Tor, the Shivering Mountain, so called because of the shale that continually fell

34

down its precipitous face, now slightly speckled with snow. The road had been closed more than once that winter and they travelled along a single track between the piled drifts. The top of the pass over into Edale was still closed, but they were able to drive nearly to its summit, and then, leaving the car, they continued their journey on foot.

From the ridge above the valley they looked down its steep sides to the village below, the houses looking like toys amid the snow. Opposite to them rose the great flank of Kinder Scout, a huge white feather bed with here and there a dark outcrop thrusting its way through the snow.

Christian would not allow them to linger, though Imogen could have spent some time absorbing the beauty of that vast panorama. He led the way to the left and they followed, along a path which had already been trampled down by other enthusiasts. There were children with toboggans and several skiers, all rejoicing in the unusual bonus of such a heavy snow-fall.

The Edge descended in a long smooth slope away from the summit upon which they stood. Christian carried over his shoulder his skis and those belonging to Lettice. Peter also had his. Teddy had been allowed to carry Imogen's pole sticks and wasted a good deal of time prodding at the snow with them. Pamela sat on the toboggan which Lettice and Joseph pulled.

When the ground began to descend, they came to a halt. Peter and Christian put on their skis, while Lettice showed Imogen how to fasten the safety straps on hers. Joseph went off with the children to find a suitable run where the ground was steeper. Lettice went to join them, and Peter glided after her, leaving Imogen standing nervously on the long runners which seemed inclined to slip away from her control.

Christian proceeded to show her how to 'walk' along a level patch. This did not prove very difficult, for she knew how to relax and her body was in perfect trim. The sticks bothered her a little until she got the hang of them. Seeing Peter at a distance, gliding around in wide arcs, she became ambitious.

'Can't I go down the slope?' she asked.

It stretched invitingly downwards, a carpet of pristine snow, except where it was scored by sledge marks. One of these had left a conveniently smooth track almost at her feet.

'No. You don't know how to stop, and there'll be bumps.'

'But I'm tired of shuffling along, and I can turn . . .'

'You think you can,' he corrected her.

Annoyed, she slid away from him, down the sledge track. Committed to the descent, she gathered speed. Supple as a willow wand, she bent her body forward, exulting in the swift motion. Engrossed in keeping her balance, she was unaware that the makers of the smooth track of hardened snow she was following had reached the top of the slope and were coming down behind her. Being heavier than she was, the toboggan was travelling faster. Its occupants yelled to her to move aside, confident that they had the right of way. The wind carried their voices away from her, and even if she had heard them, it was doubtful if she could have turned aside without falling in their path.

What happened next was over in a matter of seconds. Christian swooped upon her like an enormous bird; his arm encircled her waist, and commanding her to keep her feet together, he swerved sideways into the deep snow, supporting her weight, while the toboggan swooshed past.

Checked by the snow, into which the tips of her skis had sunk, Imogen came to a halt, painfully aware of the grip of the arm holding her up, and the man's grim face above her. Trying to free herself, she slid forward, and as he loosed his clasp, subsided upon her back.

Christian looked down at her with a glare like blue lighting.

'You little idiot! A nice mess you'd have been in if they'd run into you! I forbade you to try that slope.'

'I was doing fine,' she said defiantly. 'I'd no idea there was anything behind me. Aren't there any traffic rules at this game?'

'They expected you to get out of their way. You were on their run.'

'I didn't know that. I couldn't look behind me.'

'Even if they hadn't run into you, you'd have come to grief at the bottom. You've no real control yet and you can't expect to have it at this stage.'

'Would you mind deferring the lecture until I'm standing up?' Imogen asked acidly, feeling that he had her at a disadvantage. He was leaning on his ski-sticks looking down at her as she squatted on her skis, the better to scold her. 'I think you might at least help me up,' she went on. 'I can't manipulate these things.'

'That's obvious.'

Since he made no move to come to her aid, she tried to stand up and the skis slid forward, again precipitating her upon her rear. To her intense indignation, Christian began to laugh.

'Oh, you're hateful!' she said between her teeth.

'You must learn how to do it,' he told her. 'Make sure your skis are across the slope. Good. Now plant both your sticks on the uphill side of them.' She did so. 'Grip them with the uphill hand just above the baskets, and the downhill hand at the top. Now, draw your legs up to your body and pull yourself up on the sticks. No, girl, not like that ... edge your skis!'

The last injunction came too late. Her skis seemed to have a life of their own, they shot forward and she fell over.

'Hard luck. Try again.'

'I won't!' Covered with snow and humiliation, she

blazed up at him. 'This may be very funny for you, but I've had enough!'

She reached forward and released the safety bindings. Pushing the skis away from her, she stood up.

'I'll walk back.' She turned to face the slope.

'And leave Letty's skis behind?'

She had expected that he would carry them for her, but obviously he had no intention of doing so. Seething with fury, she picked them out of the snow and put them across her shoulder as she had seen the others do.

'Are you making me do this as a punishment for disobeying you?' she asked disdainfully. 'I think you're mean.'

'I'm not making you do anything. To walk back was your own idea,' he retorted coolly. 'You are merely facing the consequences of your own reckless conduct. And you needn't look daggers at me, you little green-eyed witch. I can't provide a ski-lift for you. They don't have them here.'

She coloured resentfully. How dared he call her a witch! Looking up, she saw with dismay the distance which she had travelled; the summit looked a long way off and there was no sign of Peter. If he had been there he would have offered to carry her gear, she was sure, but Christian was trying to revenge himself for the scare which she had given him by making the ascent as hard for her as possible. Too proud to complain, she started plodding upwards through the snow.

Christian had his own method of ascending. Enviously she watched as he ran in long traversing loops, swinging gracefully round the turns. As an exhibition of his mastery of his art, it was no doubt a superb performance, but she was in no mood to admire it.

It was a long, weary trek, though the slope was not very steep, and that she had only her own folly to blame for her predicament was no consolation. As

Christian passed and repassed her on his criss-cross journey, his fair hair lifted by the breeze. He was bare-headed, obviously enjoying himself. She decided there was no one she hated with a blacker hatred than Mr Christian Wainwright.

When at last she had made it, he slithered to a stop beside her, and to her surprise said:

'Well done! You've got grit.'

'Thanks very much,' she returned, 'but I hadn't any option, had I?'

'You could have sat down and cried. I've seen it happen.'

'Indeed? But I'm not the crying sort. What would you have done if I had?'

He leaned upon his ski-poles, considering her.

'I'm not sure. I might have slapped your face if you seemed hysterical, or I might have felt I must carry you.'

'At least you've been saved that imposition.'

'I might have found it ... quite pleasant.'

There was a wicked gleam in his blue eyes, and Imogen dropped her lashes, unable to meet them.

'If you're such a Samson, you could at least have carried my skis,' she reproached him, dropping them at his feet, while she rubbed her shoulder ruefully.

'I might,' he agreed mildly. 'I was waiting for you to ask.'

'I wouldn't do that,' she declared proudly.

'Well, you managed very well. The exercise will have toughened you.'

'Thanks again, but I didn't come here to be toughened,' she began heatedly, but at that moment Peter came gliding up to create a diversion. He asked how she had got on.

'She's hardly ready for the slalom yet,' Christian said grinning, 'but she's already tried the downhill.'

Peter looked anxious. 'You didn't let her do anything rash?'

'I couldn't stop her, she's too impetuous,' Christian told him. 'But since you've come, I'll leave her with you and see how the going is down into Edale.'

He skated off to the steeper decline on the other side of the Edge. On his way he passed the rest of the family, who had abandoned tobogganing in favour of building a snowman, and they left their labour to follow him.

'Come on,' Peter urged Imogen, 'this'll be worth seeing.'

Somewhat reluctantly she trailed after them and arrived just in time to see Christian make his descent. He shot down the almost precipitous incline at a tremendous speed. The other people on the Edge had joined the Wainwrights to watch this daring performance and there was quite a little crowd assembled on top of the hill.

He slid out across the frozen fields in the valley, a small black dot on a white sheet.

'How's he going to get back?' Teddy asked. 'It's awful steep.'

'You'll see,' his father told him.

Christian skated back to the shortest route up the decline, which was too perpendicular to traverse. He came up sideways, lifting one ski after the other, a crablike performance, and in a surprisingly short time reached the top. Imogen noticed he was not winded at all, while his audience raised a cheer.

'Perfect condition,' Peter murmured enviously from beside her. 'If only I were an athlete instead of a pen-pusher!'

Christian stood surveying the route he had followed, looking like one of his Viking ancestors who had returned from a successful raid.

'Bit bumpy,' he remarked. Then he took off his skis. The two children rushed up to him demanding that he came to admire their snowman and the whole family moved away. Imogen watched them go disconsolately. She was sick of traipsing through snow, and Peter noticed her expression.

'We'll wait here,' he said, and proceeded to scrape the snow off a rock so that she could sit down. He stripped off his anorak and spread it over the bare surface.

'Won't you be cold without it?' she asked.

'No. I was rather too warm in this sunshine.'

He was wearing a thick sweater, so possibly he spoke the truth, and Imogen sat down thankfully upon the seat he had provided, making room for him to join her.

The sun poured down upon them out of a cloudless blue sky. Imogen looked across the valley at the immaculate white waste of Kinder's bulk and had to admit that it was all very beautiful.

'Does the girl-friend ski?' she asked negligently.

'I haven't got a girl-friend.'

'I mean Christian's, the one he rang up about.'

'Oh, Erica. No. I think Christian promised her that he'd teach her.'

'Did he? He seems to want to teach all and sundry.'

'It's experience for him.'

'I bet it is.' She chuckled, thinking she had given Christian more than he had bargained for. 'Is that why, since she isn't available, he wanted to try his hand on me?'

Peter looked slightly bewildered by her acid tone.

'Didn't you enjoy it? He's supposed to be a good teacher.'

'I didn't appreciate his methods.'

'What a pity, I suppose he didn't make allowances for you being a girl.' Peter looked really worried. 'He'll have to know how to handle women if he's to succeed when he starts his ski-school.'

'Is that his intention?'

'Yes, when he gives up racing. It's time he settled to something, he's getting on for thirty.'

'A vast age,' Imogen commented, knowing Peter was twenty-two. 'But this Erica will be very disappointed, to have missed him. Their communications can't be very good if she didn't know he was coming.'

'Christian always does things upon the spur of the moment,' Peter explained, 'and she hardly ever goes away, so he thought she'd be sure to be here.'

'Is it serious?'

Peter shrugged his shoulders. 'Christian is a damned fine chap,' he said, 'but when it comes to girls, he lets himself be carried away by moonlight and a pretty face and then spends the next day wondering how he can explain that he didn't mean what he said.'

'I'd never believe anything he said,' Imogen declared emphatically. 'I've learned just how much men's pretty speeches are worth.'

An edge of bitterness had crept into her voice and Peter looked at her reproachfully.

'We aren't all like Christian,' he assured her. 'You can be certain that whatever I say to you I mean.'

'Then you must be the exception that proves the rule,' she said carelessly.

'I suppose you meet all sorts in London? Is there anybody special?'

She laughed to conceal her pain. 'No. I'm footloose and fancy-free.'

His face registered his satisfaction and she realised that she had made a mistake. She should have told him that she was committed, but it was too late to rectify her error. But if he was determined to burn his fingers, it was his look-out, she thought, hardening her heart, and she could not be held to blame.

He was gazing at her admiringly, and with the colour her exercise had brought to her cheeks, she was looking very attractive. Little tendrils of hair escaped from under her hood to frame her face, and her green eyes were bright and clear.

'I find that quite inexplicable,' he said. 'I should have thought you would have had shoals of young men queueing up to date you.'

'Perhaps I have,' she returned mischievously. 'But it doesn't follow that I'm interested. You see, Pete, I'm a mercenary minx. I'm only out for fun. I don't think I've got a heart.'

She hoped he would take the warning.

'I don't believe you,' he said earnestly. 'You can't kid me you're that sort, Imogen. It's simply that you haven't met the right man.'

Her gaze went to the snow-clad hills while pain stabbed her. She had met the right man—and lost him.

'Sorry to butt in,' Lettice said from behind them. 'But it's time we went back for dinner. We have it at midday for the children.'

She looked from Peter's self-conscious face to Imogen's aloof one with an amused expression. 'Going to join us, Pete?'

'I'd love to, but ...' His eyes sought Christian, who had come up and was watching them with a sardonic smile. 'What are you going to do?'

'Stay here while the going's good,' that gentleman announced. 'You don't mind, do you, Letty? A cold snack will do me when I come in. I don't think this weather is going to last.'

'It's a casserole and it'll warm up,' Lettice said resignedly, well knowing her stepson's casual attitude towards meals when more interesting pursuits absorbed him. 'But the forecast said the cold would continue.'

'Forecasts aren't always right, and I can smell a thaw,' he returned. 'I suppose you won't stay, Imogen?'

'I've had enough for one day,' she said hastily.

'Even though it looks like being your first and last

43

opportunity?' he asked, holding out a lean brown hand to help her to her feet.

Ignoring it, she stood up, shaking the snow from her clothes.

'There isn't much point in going on with it,' she suggested. 'I don't suppose I'll ever ski again.' Or want to, she added to herself.

She was aware that Christian was studying her speculatively, and wondered what interested him in her. She was only a stopgap for the absent Erica, and could not be looking very glamorous. She was sure her nose was shining and she wore no make-up. Perhaps he was comparing her unfavourably with Erica, for he seemed to be assessing her point by point.

Slightly disconcerted by his keen scrutiny, she turned away and began to walk back towards the car.

Peter elected to stay with Christian, who said they would return on foot so that Joseph could use the car for his family.

'Imogen has had enough walking, I think,' he said with a sly glance at her averted face. She would like to have slapped him.

'Christian spent a lot of time with you,' Lettice remarked curiously, when they were all installed in the car.

'I didn't ask him to,' Imogen snapped, 'it was his idea.' She was not going to admit that most of the time had been spent in walking back up Rushup Edge. Vaguely she wondered if Erica had ever sat and cried when Christian had demanded too much of her, and if he had carried her home. The thought was strangely unwelcome.

Lettice was laughing. 'Pete didn't like it at all,' she said. 'You've made a conquest there, my dear.'

'Oh, for crying out loud!' Imogen exclaimed with exasperation. 'I haven't known him a week.'

'Ever heard of love at first sight?' Joseph asked from

behind the steering wheel.

'Yes, in books and plays, but never in real life,' Imogen retorted. 'Peter's only suffering from growing pains, he's not grown up yet.'

'He's older than you are,' Lettice pointed out, gently, 'and growing pains can hurt.'

Teddy piped up, 'What's growing pains, Mummy? Have I got any?'

Lettice proceeded to give her son an explanation involving what was probably rheumatism, while Imogen thought she was jumping to conclusions. Peter might have a fancy for her, but it could only be a fancy in so short a time and she did not expect to stay in Derbyshire longer than about a couple of weeks. If he persisted in pursuing her during her stay, a little mild flirtation might create a pleasant diversion, but there was no reason why it should prove more durable than most holiday romances. Peter, she judged, was more sentimental than passionate and would soon forget her when she had gone.

The young men did not return until it was getting dark, and Peter being exhausted went straight home. Christian seemed as fresh as he had been in the morning and ate an enormous meal in the kitchen, which did not deter him from joining the family for high tea an hour later.

Rain clouds were gathering in the west and there was a definite rise in temperature. The weather report confirmed that they had been mistaken earlier and a thaw was on the way.

'Thank goodness for that!' Lettice exclaimed. 'But I suppose you'll be disappointed, Christian?'

'Not really, only for Peter's sake,' he replied. 'The skiing here is hardly up to my standard.'

'But you'll be horribly bored without any.'

'Not at all. There are plenty of other diversions.' His glance flickered over Imogen.

45

She met it with a little stir of her pulses, which should perhaps have warned her, but she was convinced that Ray's defection had left her invulnerable to masculine advances. She did not like Christian any better upon closer acquaintance, but he was exciting and stimulating. He was much more fun than poor Peter, she decided, and if he was contemplating amusing himself with her, she had no objection to playing along with him until the time came to part, and then she would tell him exactly what she thought of him, which would not be at all what he expected to hear. Anticipation of the game ahead made her green eyes sparkle and her smile provoking. He, she was sure, could not be hurt, he had no more intention than she had of becoming seriously involved. She could go as far as she liked without having to consider his susceptibilities, as she did with Peter and the absent Erica had better hurry up and come home if she wanted to claim her property. Possibly she was doing the girl a kindness by annexing her young man if he had no serious intentions towards her as Peter had averred.

Vivian's advice was beginning to bear fruit. Rightly she had declared that men were fun, and it was a new role for Imogen to try her skill at playing with fire.

CHAPTER THREE

THAT evening as they sat in front of a log fire, pleasantly relaxed after the children were in bed, Imogen heard more about Greta Olssen.

'She hasn't been at all well,' Christian told them, having seen his sister recently. 'Jamtland is too cold for her in winter. She wants to sell the farm and move down to Stockholm, where she can get a job if she can find someone to look after the children. I shall be going over to see her and help her to settle up her affairs.'

Imogen barely listened. Greta in remote Sweden was only a name to her, she had no premonition that she would one day be much more. She wondered idly if the girl were like her brother. She must be a handsome woman if she were, and since they were twins it was more than likely.

'I haven't seen my grandchildren since they were babies,' Joseph said, after expressing his relief that Christian was going to see his daughter who, he felt, was very much on her own. 'Let me see—Sven, the boy, must be nearly five now. Perhaps next summer?' He looked questioningly at Lettice.

'I don't see why not,' Lettice agreed. 'But summer is still a long way off, and it doesn't arrive in mid-Sweden until June.'

'Poor Greta!' Joseph exclaimed, and Imogen echoed him. The place must have a dreadful climate.

As Christian had predicted, the thaw arrived that night in an outbreak of heavy rain. Sunday was dull and cold, causing some anxiety about floods in the valleys, as the melted snow came down from the hills, but it still lay on the higher peaks.

Imogen went with Lettice and the children to church. She had fulfilled their anticipations on the previous day by offering her small gifts which were rather overshadowed by Christian's much more expensive ones. Peter came in during the afternoon with books and maps for Imogen to study. Next weekend he was planning to take her upon some expeditions to see the country, since the roads looked like being clear. He expressed insincere regret that his car was too small to accommodate the whole family. The Wainwrights did not possess one.

'But I can take the lot of you in my station-wagon,' Christian said mischievously, watching Peter's face fall.

'Will you still be here?'

'I expect so.'

'Well, that's great,' Peter said unenthusiastically.

Christian went on: 'If there's no more snow, we might run through the Dales and finish up at Matlock. Riber Reserve is open all the year round and the kids would like to see the animals.'

'It's a long way,' Lettice said doubtfully.

'Mine's a fast car.'

The children became wildly excited at the prospect.

'Will there be lions, Chris?' Teddy demanded.

'No, but they have a wildcat and a couple of bears.'

Imogen had experienced an unworthy glow of gratification. Christian had stymied Peter's attempt to monopolise her. It looked as though he was a rival for her favours in spite of Erica. This was the sort of balm that would quickest heal the wound Raymond had dealt to her vanity. Without any desire to become personally involved, she was enjoying the cat-and-dog looks the two young men were throwing at each other.

Peter said sulkily: 'I should have thought Imogen would have had enough of the children by next Saturday.'

'Why shouldn't they have a treat too?' Christian asked blandly. 'I don't do a lot for them. If she's bored, you can entertain Imogen while I show them round.'

Both Imogen and Peter shot him a puzzled look. Why after preventing an expedition alone, was he now suggesting they should keep together? Or possibly, Imogen thought, he was so sure of his charms he did not believe that with himself present, she could bear to go off with Peter.

With a little provocative smile curling her lips, she said: 'I think we should all stick together, and I'd like to see Teddy and Pam's reaction to the bears and the wildcat.'

The week that followed was sunny and frosty, which augured well for the Riber expedition. For the next two days, Imogen helped Lettice about the house in the mornings, hindered by Pam, for Teddy went to school. Joseph and Peter were at work, Peter in Chinley, Joseph in Hope. Christian came and went, and Imogen wondered if Erica Brayshaw had returned, but if she had, he did not mention her, and neither did Lettice.

On the second afternoon, Christian asked Imogen to come for a walk up the Winnats. Lettice could not come as she had to meet Teddy from school, and Imogen was glad of the diversion.

The Pass was approached by a private road, which had once been the main highway. On either side, grey cliffs soared above it. It was, Christian told her, a favourite place for picnickers in summer, and rambling clubs. The ascent was very steep in places, though cars could and did pass up and down.

'Must have been a bit of a grind for the old coaches,' Christian remarked. 'In those days there was no other road, and the rocks were good cover for robbers and highwaymen.'

Imogen looked up at the tall sinister crags on either

hand, and shivered.

'Must have been eerie when it was getting dark.'

'Particularly when the wind howls down the Pass, and it does howl ... like lost souls.'

The Pass ended on the high ground above it, and looking back she could see how the split rocks formed a natural gorge in the hill side.

Walking back by the main road, under the lee of Mam Tor, he asked her if she would like to see one of the caverns, the Treak or the Blue John mines.

'Treak Cliff hill is the only known source of Blue John spa in the world,' he told her.

'I've heard a lot about Blue John, but what exactly is it?' she asked.

'Calcium fluoride, coloured by films of oil deposited on the face of the crystals; bitumen, as oxidised oil seeps through the rocks of the hill in sections. In fact oil has actually been extracted from the spa.'

But when they reached the huts which marked the entrance to the caves, they found they were not officially open until Easter. Unperturbed, Christian had a long argument with one of the guides, who knew him well; some money changed hands, with the result that he agreed to take them inside.

They traversed long passages tunnelled through the rock, descended slimy stairs, the whole lit by strings of electric bulbs. The Treak had in addition to the still unworked veins of Blue John, a number of stalactites and stalagmites. Of these there was a good collection in the furthermost cave, forming a lacy pattern, illuminated by electric bulbs placed strategically behind them. The caves themselves were natural.

Imogen did not altogether enjoy the expedition into the heart of the mountain; she was very much aware of the tons of rock above her head, and it was with relief that she stumbled out into the light of day.

'These hills are all honeycombed with caverns,'

Christian told her, 'complete with underground rivers. You must see the Speedwell, which is a flooded mine-shaft and you travel along it in a boat. At the end, the astonished miners came upon a great fall of water which stopped their progress, a river coming from God knows where and going no one knows whence.'

'A sort of Styx?' she suggested nervously. 'I don't think I like caves very much, they give me claustrophobia.'

They were descending the long flight of steps that led from the caverns to the road, and they were slippery with frost.

'Careful,' Christian warned, and put his arm round her to steady her.

'I'm being very careful.' She smiled provocatively up into the brown face so near her own. 'I'm always very careful. I hope you are too.'

She was a little surprised by the ease with which the flippant words, with a hint of a double meaning, came off her tongue. Christian's encircling arm did not disconcert her, in fact she was enjoying his proximity. Delicious little thrills ran up her spine. Sexually he was very attractive, but she knew from experience how transitory such attraction was. Only when it was joined with love could it develop into a lasting tie, and Christian, she felt sure, had a contempt as great as her own and Vivien's for love.

He was looking down into her eyes with an amused glint in his.

'Now what precisely do you mean by that?'

'That I never go very far.'

'Thanks for the caution,' he observed lightly, then added more seriously, 'I hope you won't make an exception of Pete.'

'Oh, Pete!' They had reached the bottom of the steps and she threw off his arm impatiently. She did not want to be reminded of Peter.

'That boy's vulnerable,' he told her.

She wanted to cry, so was I once, and I was wounded. Instead she said callously: 'That's his look-out.'

'He's not used to the ways of smart dames from the swinging city.'

'Then why don't you warn him?'

'He wouldn't take it from me. He'd think I was jealous.'

'And are you?' she asked, looking at him sideways.

'I don't think I've any cause to be.'

Insufferable! she thought; he believed he could take her from Peter at the drop of a hat, if he wanted to, but did he want to? She peered up at him from under her lashes and smiled seductively.

'I can play that game too,' he told her, his eyes kindling, 'but Pete doesn't realise that it's only a game.'

'Then he'll have to learn, won't he?' she asked sweetly.

'I'm asking you to leave him alone.'

That was unfair. She had avoided being alone with Peter as much as possible and she had tried to discourage him, but Christian apparently had not noticed her efforts. In any case it was not his business.

'Have you constituted yourself his keeper?' she asked scornfully. 'I don't think he would thank you. I believe he's over twenty-one and out of leading strings.'

'But for all that he's a country boy, and simple.'

'And you, of course, are far from simple?'

'I'm older and more experienced. I warn you, Imogen, if you make Pete suffer you'll have me to reckon with.'

'How dramatic!' she scoffed. 'And what do you imagine you could do to me?'

She met his blue gaze and hastily looked away. There was something in its depths which made her heart flutter.

'You'll see,' he returned coldly.

'I'm not frightened by empty threats,' she said defiantly, 'and I don't think Peter Lethwaite is quite the nit you're trying to make out.'

Unexpectedly he asked: 'Have you ever been in love?'

'Love's a myth,' she said bitterly. 'A romantic fantasy.'

She saw his face was grave, and he was looking at her commiseratingly.

'I think you have at some time been hurt very badly.'

She winced. He was the last person in whom she could bring herself to confide. If she judged him aright, he was as frivolous and hard-boiled as she was trying to become. If she told him about Ray, he would think she was the sort of soft, sentimental fool whom he could dupe at his will. She stopped on the roadside and looked at him out of eyes narrowed to green slits.

'I can't help your thoughts,' she said coolly. 'But you can get straight about me. You're quite, quite wrong. Nobody has ever hurt me. Nobody ever can. I've always been, and I always will be, a good-time girl. I take all I can get, and I give ... nothing.'

She walked on down the road, her head held high, and he said softly:

'What a very unpleasant character you've given yourself!'

'It's what I am. I'm being honest with you.'

He smiled dryly. 'Is that a compliment—or a warning?'

'Take it how you please.'

The turn in the road brought the town into sight, and she went on scornfully:

'You seem very anxious to protect your friend from my wicked wiles, but are you any better than I am? What about your girl-friends? Aren't any of them vulnerable too?'

'Who's been talking about my girl-friends?' he asked, amused. 'How do you know I've got any?'

'It would be extraordinary if you hadn't, and your family said...' She floundered, trying to remember what had been said, and remembered that it was Peter who had dubbed him a philanderer. 'There's Erica,' she said triumphantly.

He laughed easily. 'A good-timer like yourself, so there are no bones broken.'

'You asked for her when you first rang up,' she reminded him.

'So I did. I had her in mind for something...' He broke off to ask. 'By the way, have you any job lined up for your return to town?'

The sudden switch in the conversation made her blink, and she said without thinking:

'Nothing at all.' Then catching his speculative look, she added hastily, 'I'm hoping my agent will have found something for me.'

'Yours is a very uncertain profession,' he observed.

'I've got a home to go to if I'm out of work,' she returned.

'So you don't mind sponging on your parents?'

She did mind and hoped devoutly that she would not have to do so, but he was being offensive by mentioning it.

'That's my affair,' she said stiffly.

'Sorry, I didn't mean to be rude. I was only thinking that if the theatricals fall through you might be glad to take up some other type of employment if the salary was satisfactory.'

'I don't want to do anything except dancing,' she insisted.

'Then I hope you'll end by being Pavlova the Second, but just in case you change your mind, I know of a position which might suit you.'

'The one you were going to offer Erica?'

'I think you might be more suitable.'

'If that's intended as a compliment it's a very backhand one, and I don't think any position which you had to offer would appeal to me.'

He smiled serenely at this rudeness. 'You don't know what it is, and I can be very persuasive.'

'I don't doubt it.' He said no more, but her curiosity was roused, and she asked: 'What is it?'

He gave her a quizzical look. 'Since you're not interested, I'd be wasting my breath by expounding.'

'You said you could be very persuasive,' she reminded him archly.

'So you might consider it—whatever it is?'

She looked at him doubtfully. 'How can I say until I know what I'm in for?'

He laughed. 'Sorry to disappoint you, but it is by no means amorous, quite the reverse. But there are some details to be considered first.'

'Hadn't you better get my consent before you do that?' Imogen suggested.

'Not at all. I want to present you with a completed proposition, so if you refuse, it'll be in order for the next one.'

'Meaning you've others lined up?'

'Naturally. You don't imagine you're unique?'

'No, of course not.' But she was chagrined. 'Oh well, I don't suppose it's anything I'd want to do,' she went on, and glanced at him slyly, hoping he would become more informative, but he said nothing, which was all the more aggravating.

Lettice was astonished when she heard that they had been down the Treak.

'It isn't open yet.'

'Amazing what a little bribery will do,' Christian observed.

'And you of course have a way with you,' Lettice said admiringly.

'Perhaps, when I want something,' Christian agreed. 'But it was money and cajolery thrown away. Imogen got claustrophobia.'

'I enjoyed it very much,' she said hastily, fearing that she had been ungracious. 'It was most interesting. Thank you for everything, even the offer you haven't made.'

'All in good time,' he told her lazily. 'I'm waiting for the psychological moment.'

And although Lettice demanded to know what they were talking about, neither would enlighten her.

The next morning Christian went to London for a few days, to contact his sports organisation. Imogen was dismayed to discover how much she missed him. She explained this to herself by insisting that his was such a strong personality that it was not surprising that his absence could be felt and she was in reality relieved to be free of him; she was also a little bored. Whatever else Christian was, he was never dull. She wondered what it was he wanted her to do. He had been maddeningly evasive about it, but she had to admit he was clever. He had deliberately aroused her curiosity and refused to satisfy it. However he had overreached himself, for upon reflection she determined that whatever it was she would have no part in it. He was becoming too disturbing to her peace of mind, and in spite of her boasted immunity to male charm, she was not at all sure she could cope with him.

Peter joined them in the evening, but she avoided any intimate talk with him, by saying she wanted to watch the play on television. This was a Shakespeare production, *Much Ado About Nothing*, and the song in it seemed to have a personal message for her.

Sigh no more ladies, sigh no more.
Men were deceivers ever;

> *One foot in sea, and one on shore,*
> *To one thing constant never.*
> *Then sigh not so,*
> *But let them go,*
> *And be you blithe and bonny.*

Men were deceivers all, and she would sigh after none of them, neither Raymond nor Christian, but let them go. Shakespeare knew what he was writing about.

Christian did not return until late on Friday night, and as when he had first arrived, Imogen was in bed. To her annoyance she could not sleep until she heard the sound of his voice in the hall. The children had been worried by his continued absence, seeing in it a threat to the promised trip to Riber next day. She assured herself that it was anxiety upon their account that had kept her listening for his coming.

They were lucky in their weather. The sun shone brightly and except upon the heights of Kinder the snow had gone. There was plenty of room in the estate wagon for all of them. The children reposed on cushions in the back, Lettice sat beside Christian, and Imogen between Joseph and Peter on the rear seat.

Their way lay through white limestone dales, gorges along the valley bottoms, between windswept uplands, across treeless moors, and passed grey-stone villages, Christian going out of his way to show them the scenery.

Riber Castle was neither old nor historical, having been built no earlier than 1862, and was an ugly example of a rich man's folly. Erected around a central square, most of the interior had fallen into disrepair, but the imposing corner towers still stood, together with their connecting walls.

But it was built on a magnificent site. It stood upon a high ridge above the Derwent Valley and was a landmark for miles around. Below it, Matlock was spread out like a map, and the winding road, river and railway down to Matlock Bath could be clearly traced. High Tor and its opposite ridge were dwarfed by the height of Riber, and even the tree-clad rise of Masson Hill looked insignificant.

Imogen was enraptured by the tremendous panorama before her, and could hardly tear herself away to visit the animals, for the place had been taken over by a group of zoologists, who had turned the grounds into a fauna reserve. There were a great many varieties of birds, otters, beavers, the promised bears, restlessly roaming their enclosure, foxes and the wildcat, which was disappointingly curled up asleep and looked like a domestic pussy.

Lettice had brought a picnic lunch which they ate in the car, since it was too cold to sit out of doors, and the hot coffee in the thermos flasks was more than welcome.

When they had finished, they continued their explorations, and Peter made several attempts to dislodge Imogen from the others, but she remained firmly anchored to the children. Teddy obligingly developed a desire for her company, giving her a surprising amount of information about the animals they were looking at. Christian was monopolised by his small half-sister, who every now and then demanded to be carried, a weakness Lettice deplored when Christian acceded to it.

'After all, her legs are very short,' he told his stepmother, and against his own long length this was very apparent.

Imogen was aware of his eyes upon her more than once and saw him glance from her to the sulky Peter with a sardonic smile, but he made no attempt to come near her himself.

Teddy expressed a wish to explore the quadrangle in the middle of the castle, and going in through an ungated entrance they found themselves surrounded by the four sides of the great dilapidated building, most of which was boarded up, with signs saying it was unsafe to enter it. A pair of black ravens flapping around added to its air of desolation.

'Can't we go inside?' Teddy asked.

'No. It's too dangerous.'

The child was disappointed and rather overawed by his surroundings and agreed without reluctance to go back outside.

As they reached the entrance, Peter came through.

'Hurry up,' he told Teddy. 'You'll be just in time to see the otters fed.'

Imogen would have followed him as he rushed off, but Peter barred her way.

'Don't go. I've had no time with you at all. You seemed quite absorbed in those tiresome kids.'

'I like children,' she said defensively.

'Meaning you prefer their society to mine?'

'Nothing of the sort. Don't be touchy. It is after all their treat.' She did not want to hurt him, neither did she want to encourage him. Christian's warning had made a deeper impression than she wanted to admit. Peter deserved at least sincerity.

They were standing just within the courtyard, concealed from the outside by a pile of fallen masonry.

'Can you deny you've been avoiding me?' he asked accusingly.

'It's for your own good,' she told him. 'You see, I'm not your sort of girl at all. You don't really know me.'

'I know you better than you think,' he insisted.

'You're idealising me,' she said gently. 'I'm shallow and a bit of a flirt. I only want a good time.'

'You're trying to put me off. Good-time girls don't come to places like Castleton, they don't devote themselves to children. I've watched you with Pam and Teddy.'

She shook her head, smiling ruefully. 'They're just a change. I came up here because I hadn't been very well...' She swallowed painfully, remembering what had been a worse calamity than the measles, but she could not mention that to Peter, any more than she could to Christian, but for a different reason. It would destroy the heartless image which she was trying to present to him. He might even imagine he could catch her on the rebound.

'Soon I'll be going back to London,' she went on lightly. 'The bright lights and ... and bottle parties. That's my real setting. You'd hate the sort of life I enjoy.'

He looked at her doubtfully.

'I don't believe you're really like that,' he said slowly. 'The real reason why you're brushing me off is Christian.'

'Christian?' She laughed merrily. 'Oh really, Pete, I've hardly seen him, and I'm not impressed by his athletic feats. He's the last person I'd ever fall for—besides, there's Erica, isn't there?'

His mouth set obstinately. He was unconvinced because he believed his friend was irresistible to men and women alike.

'Too bad he had to come back while you were here,' he complained.

'His coming makes no difference at all,' she assured him. 'Please, Pete, do understand. I like you as a friend, but I've nothing to give you except friendship.'

'You despise me,' he said angrily, 'because I'm only an office worker, but I'll show you ...'

She laid a hand on his arm. 'Hush, it's not that at all.'

His own hand closed convulsively over hers on his arm, preventing her from withdrawing it.

'We'd better join the others,' she told him gently.

'No, not yet.'

She turned her head aside as pulling her closer he tried to kiss her, and saw Christian watching them from the entry. She jerked herself away from Peter, as he spoke to them, angrily aware that she had blushed.

'Letty sent me to find you,' he told them. 'She thinks it's time we started for home.'

Peter gave a reckless laugh, and went up to his friend with something of a swagger.

'I say, old man, if the weather holds up tomorrow, what about a little rock-climbing? I've always wanted to have a go at the quarry on the south side of Combes Moss, but I've been waiting until you could come with me.'

Christian looked at the boy anxiously, sensing some sort of compulsion urging him on to an act of bravado.

'Why, so I did,' he admitted. 'If you really want to go there tomorrow, we'll talk about it this evening.'

Which presumably they did, for Christian went home with Peter and Imogen did not see either of them again that night.

'I didn't know Derbyshire was a climbing area,' she said to Joseph during the evening.

'Didn't you? Of course we've nothing very great. The Lake District and Wales have higher rock-climbs, but we've great variety. In the north and east are the gritstone edges, and in the south and west you'll find limestone crags with plenty of steep, hard climbing, including Chee Tor itself. We call them the White Peak, as opposed to the Black Peak, but limestone is not for the inexperienced. Want to have a go?'

'No, but I just wondered.'

'I suppose Christian has been talking about it. He's done most of the rock-climbs about here.'

She wondered if there was any feat Christian did not do, but Joseph's assurance of his competence was reassuring. She had a suspicion that Peter wanted to do something spectacular to impress her, but if he was in

Christian's company, he would be quite safe. Somewhere along the line, her inclination to flirt with Peter had evaporated. He was, as Christian had said, too vulnerable, and her heart was not in it, or more correctly it was in it. That inconvenient organ, the existence of which she had tried so hard to ignore, insisted it would be too unkind. Vivien might be able to find pleasure in leading on amorous males and then repudiating them, but she was beginning to realise that she could never imitate Vivien. She could not take out Raymond's defection upon Peter.

Her stay was drawing to a close; she could not trespass much longer upon the Wainwrights' hospitality, and she was quite well enough now to look for another job. She would fix a date for her departure and never see Peter again.

Yet she felt extremely reluctant to leave Barley Howe. She assured herself that it was because she dreaded returning to London and reopening old wounds. But Raymond's image was beginning to dim. It could not be, she insisted feverishly, that another man's was becoming imposed upon it, neither could it be possible that her reluctance to leave was due to the fact that she did not want to say goodbye to Christian. The idea was absurd. She would miss him of course, 'more than I want him', she told herself wryly, but as for any tenderer feeling...? She decided that it would be as well to go soon.

Sunday was bright after a frost and Imogen again went to church with the family. The two young men had gone off together in Christian's car, though Lettice had remarked that she would not have expected the rocks to be in very good condition after so much snow, but her husband laughed and pooh-poohed her anxiety. Christian was much too old a hand to take any risks.

In the late afternoon, Christian rang up and asked

them to fetch the Lethwaites to the telephone, for they had not got one. While Lettice ran next door, he gave his news to Joseph. There had been an accident and Peter was in Buxton hospital.

'How serious is it?' Imogen asked anxiously, when Mrs Lethwaite had come running to the telephone and Joseph joined her in the sitting-room.

'A broken leg and possibly other injuries.' Joseph looked worried, and Imogen was assailed by a pang of guilt. She had felt all along that something like this was going to happen, but she could not have stopped Peter from making the climb, and she felt impatient with the silly boy who had brought so great a calamity upon himself for so futile a reason.

Christian came back late in the evening. Peter, he said, was comfortable, but he did not enlarge upon the accident, in spite of Letty's anxious questions. They did gather that Peter had acted recklessly, refusing to use a rope.

'So unlike him!' Lettice exclaimed. 'He's usually so cautious.'

'Quite,' Christian said with a snap, 'and he thinks caution isn't daring enough.' He looked at Imogen. 'Could I have a word with you—alone?'

Surprised, she followed him into the hall. He led the way thence into the kitchen and shut the door, leaning against it.

'Peter has asked for you,' he said abruptly. 'I promised him I'd bring you to see him tomorrow.'

Imogen looked at him in consternation. 'If he really wants to see me, I'll have to go,' she began hesitantly, 'but...'

'But what?' The question was like a pistol shot.

'I ... I didn't want to get involved with him,' she blurted out. 'If I go to him in hospital, what will his people think?'

'What the hell does it matter what they think?'

Christian exploded. 'Peter fell because he was trying to show off, for your benefit.'

'But I wasn't even there...'

'You'd have been told about it. He was trying to prove to you and himself that he was as good a man as ... shall we say, myself?'

'But it isn't fair to blame me,' Imogen exclaimed. 'I'd nothing to do with it.'

'Pardon me, you'd everything to do with it.'

'I don't agree. I don't particularly admire athletic feats, it all seems rather a waste of energy which could be more usefully employed.'

It was not until she saw his odd expression that she realised her words applied also to himself, but she was not going to apologise. It would do him good to know there was at least one person who was not impressed by his gold medal.

'Be that as it may,' he said shortly, 'you can't pretend you haven't been leading Pete on.'

'You don't know that. You haven't been here, and he can't be serious about me, he's only known me a week.'

'Boys of his age can become infatuated overnight,' Christian remarked from the superiority of his seven additional years. 'You've all the glamour for him of being on the stage and coming from a great city.' His voice was coldly mocking. 'If only he knew what little bitches actresses can be! You know perfectly well you've been leading him up the garden, without, of course, having any intention of satisfying him in any sort of way. It amused you to play upon his emotions.'

'No, Christian, you're wrong.' Now he had put what she called to herself the Vivien motive into actual words, it sounded bald and unpleasant, he was accusing her of being the kind of girl which she had told him she was, but now she found she wanted to revoke that image, to make him understand that she was not

64

as black as she had painted herself to him. 'It didn't amuse me at all. I tried to put him off. I even told him I was what you so charmingly described as a bitch.'

'Indeed? Was that what you were trying to do at Riber?'

'Yes. I was giving him the brush-off.'

She remembered that Christian had appeared at just the wrong moment, when Peter was holding her, and his face expressed his disbelief of her explanation.

'It didn't look that way to me,' he said drily. 'But whatever you were up to, you'll come with me to Buxton tomorrow if I have to drag you there by your hair.'

He would too, she thought, noticing the implacable set of his jaw.

'Of course I'll come, if you think I should,' she said frankly. 'I never said I would not.'

'You hesitated—started to make excuses.'

'That was because I don't want to raise hopes which I can't fulfil.'

'Bit late in the day to think of that,' he observed. He gave her an enigmatical look. 'Why can't you fulfil his hopes? What's wrong with Pete?'

'Nothing, he's a nice boy, but I'm not in the least in love with him.'

'I doubt if you're capable of loving wholeheartedly,' he told her with a slight sneer, but the intent, almost questioning look in his eyes belied his words.

'I don't want to,' she flung at him. 'Love can be painful.'

'That I wouldn't know, not having experienced it. Unfortunately Pete is hurt, both emotionally and physically.'

'That's why I'm trying to think what is my best course so as not to hurt him any more,' she said earnestly.

'That's obvious, isn't it? Go to him in hospital, and be kind—if you can.'

He must think that things had gone a lot further between Peter and herself than they had, she decided, and it was hopeless to try to convince him otherwise.

'If that's all,' she said quietly, 'let's end this. I'm quite prepared to go to the hospital tomorrow, but can't I get a train or a bus?'

'You could, but it's a roundabout journey, and would waste a lot of time. Is my company so obnoxious to you?'

'It is when you talk as you've been doing.'

He laughed. 'You don't like home-truths?' He came away from the door and loomed over her. 'Men are just fun to you, aren't they? You're one of the swinging girls, only out for kicks. I suppose Pete isn't exciting enough for you.'

Swift anger welled up in her; he was being intolerable!

'Men can take very good care of themselves,' she told him bitterly. 'They deserve all they get.'

'Even a broken leg?' he asked derisively, and her anger died. She had not been thinking of Peter when she spoke.

He placed his hands upon her shoulders, looking down at her with a gleam in his eyes that disconcerted her.

'You're a damnable little witch,' he told her. 'I don't wonder Pete's fallen for you, but he's no match for you, poor kid. Your kind needs a master.'

She twisted free from under his hands and with all her strength hit him hard across his sneering mouth.

His reaction was swift and merciless. There was no escape from those iron arms, neither could she evade the hard, insistent lips. When he released her she fell back against the kitchen table, her eyes blazing with outrage.

'How dare you!' she spat at him.

'Oh, I dare, I'm not afraid of little tiger cats, but

neither will I permit them to scratch me.'

Imogen clenched her hands. 'I hate you! I despise you!'

'Reciprocated.' His eyes were alight with mischief. 'Or more correctly I haven't any feelings about you at all.'

'Then why did you...' she started, and broke off. She had been going to say, 'kiss me', but it occurred to her his action had been committed more to punish her than for any other reason, and her rage was the reaction that he had expected. Instantly she changed her tactics; she would not let him have the satisfaction of enjoying her indignation.

'Your methods are a bit crude,' she said coolly. 'They may give your country girls a kick, but I'm used to a more subtle technique.'

He raised an eyebrow. 'The basic element is always the same.'

'Sex?' she suggested, and hoped she sounded sophisticated.

'Well, of course,' he said with a drawl. 'That's all there could ever be between you and me, though you'll have to warm up a bit for it to be successful. However, I don't suppose you're always such an icicle.'

She moved away to the sink and started to run the hot tap, aware that she was not nearly as calm as she wanted to appear. Her heart was beating erratically and she was very conscious of his masculine presence which seemed to pervade the small room. Very deliberately she washed her face and mouth.

'I get the message,' he told her. 'Doubtless I lack the expertise of your City friends, being only a rough athlete. At a guess I should say you favour exotic Latin types with all the flowery approach of the Romance races, however insincere they are.'

Memories shook her. Raymond had been dark as a Latin, and he had known how to make himself pleasing to a woman with small courtesies and attentions, which meant nothing at all. She stifled a sigh, remembering that men were deceivers ever and she would sigh no more over any one of them—Raymond or Christian.

'I don't think this conversation is getting us anywhere,' she said coldly. 'Shall we go back into the sitting-room?'

'Certainly.' He opened the door for her with a flourish. 'At least I know exactly where I stand.'

Lettice looked at them curiously as they came in.

'You've been a long time,' she remarked.

Christian gave her an impish grin.

'Imogen had a daft idea of going to Buxton by train, I've been persuading her that it would be much easier by car, and she could trust my—driving,' he told her, with the slightest pause before the last word.

Joseph took this remark at its face value.

'Christian is an exceptionally good driver,' he assured Imogen solemnly. 'Though he travels fast, he's careful. Didn't he get us to Riber all in one piece? You need have no qualms.'

'I have none whatever about his ability in that direction,' Imogen retorted, and Lettice gave her a long look.

Imogen sat down as far away from Christian as possible and assiduously gave her attention to the television programme, an unnecessary precaution, for Christian did not even look at her for the rest of the evening, and his 'Good night' was perfunctory.

Imogen was apprehensive about her visit to the hospital. She feared that finding Peter weak and wounded, her pity might lead her into making rash promises which she could not fulfil. To add to her discomfort, Christian watched her throughout the morning with the air of a grim gaoler, as if he expected her to make an attempt to escape the ordeal at the last moment.

She had resigned herself to the inevitability of accepting his escort. The Wainwrights took it for granted that she would be going with him and she could think of no good reason to give them for refusing. Her tentative suggestion that the Lethwaites might be going was met with the information that they had stayed overnight in Buxton.

It was a bright, windy afternoon when they set forth, though there was a fresh sprinkling of snow on the top of the hills. Christian named some of them as they went through Chapel-en-le-Frith—a name, he said, which meant Chapel in the Forest, Chinley Churn, Southhead, Eccles Pike and Combes Moss. He talked impersonally about their surroundings as if the scene in the kitchen had never taken place, and gradually she thawed towards him. Though she had not wanted his company, there was no point in sulking about it.

Peter was in the General Ward, one leg in plaster, a bandage round his head. He greeted her shyly, as Christian brought her in and they presented their offerings of fruit, flowers and magazines. Then Christian withdrew, telling her she would find him outside at the end of the visiting period.

A pretty nurse came to take the flowers, and Imogen noticed that Peter's eyes followed her as she walked away down the ward.

'She's nice, that one,' he told her, 'full of fun when Sister isn't looking.'

'She's very pretty,' Imogen remarked, wondering if Peter's susceptible heart was already straying towards another object. It would be a great relief to her if that were so.

'But not like you,' Peter said with a sigh. 'It was good of you to come, Imogen. I don't deserve it. I've been such a fool.'

'We can't help accidents,' she observed brightly.

'But I could have helped this one. I did an idiotic

thing. I knew the rock was crumbling. Thank God I didn't let Christian rope himself to me. I might have pulled him down too. As it was I fell almost before he'd started, with a large piece of the hill on top of me.'

'Hard luck,' she said inadequately.

'No, sheer awkwardness, but somehow I didn't care . . .'

'It's over now,' she cut in hastily. 'When are you coming home?'

'Tomorrow or the day after. With my leg in plaster, I can hobble about on crutches. So unromantic!'

'What does it matter? You should be thankful to be alive.'

He made a grimace. 'I wouldn't have cared if I'd ended it all.'

'You're being absurd,' she told him vigorously. 'You're young, Pete, you've all your life before you.'

But she understood his feelings. She would have liked to end it all when Raymond had left her, but she had known Ray for most of her life, whereas Peter had only just met her.

'I'm not really a coward,' he said suddenly, 'but I know I can't compete with Christian.'

'Why should you want to?' she asked with exasperation. 'To excel at sport isn't everything by any means, and you're a much nicer character than he is.'

'Thanks, but it isn't the nice characters who appeal to girls,' he said disconsolately.

Imogen wanted to shake him. His obsession with her and Christian, and Christian's with Peter and her, were ridiculous. Neither had any foundation in fact. Trying to speak cheerfully, she said:

'Oh, come off it, Pete—do you want to be a Casanova? Some day you'll meet a nice girl who will appreciate all your good qualities.'

'Which you don't.'

'But I do.' Forgetting all about the cynical armour in which she had sought to enwrap herself since Raymond had let her down, she added distressfully:

'Pete dear, I'd love you if I could, but you know you can't love to order. I don't think I can love anyone again.'

'Again?' he took her up sharply.

With an effort she recovered her poise and smiled sadly.

'I didn't mean to let that out, it's an old story and painful. But you deserve a girl's first love and there are lots of charming girls about—that little nurse for one.'

As she had intended, his thoughts were directed to the other girl.

'She's rather sweet, isn't she?' he asked.

'A perfect lamb, and perhaps she has a soft spot for you. The way she looked at you!' Imogen tried to recall how the nurse had looked when she had taken the flowers; she had certainly smiled with more than professional warmth.

She was thankful when the bell rang for the visitors to depart, and in her relief, she made many rash promises to help cheer Peter's convalescence when he came home.

I knew how it would be, she thought despairingly as she walked out of the ward, turning at the door to wave to the watching Peter. Now if I'm always going to see him, Christian will accuse me of encouraging him, and if I don't he'll think I'm heartless. What is a girl to do?

Significantly she was thinking of Christian's reactions, not Peter's.

CHAPTER FOUR

IMOGEN came out into the sunny forecourt of the hospital with a sense of relief at having performed a difficult duty.

Christian was waiting for her, leaning negligently against the side of his car smoking a cigarette. She saw him before he noticed her, his head being in profile, the fine features clear-cut against a background of distant hills. He was looking towards them with a faraway expression, dreaming no doubt of future triumphs, she thought a little scornfully, not recognising that her antagonism towards those events was the natural feminine reaction towards an absorbing interest which excluded her sex.

When she had entered the car, he turned it towards the town centre, remarking:

'You'll be wanting a cup of tea after that ordeal.'

He was right, but she did not wish to drink it with him.

'I'd rather go straight back,' she said stiffly.

'But I want to discuss that proposition I mentioned.'

Any curiosity which she had felt about that had faded since the episode in the kitchen.

'It would be a waste of time,' she said cuttingly. 'Nothing you proposed could have the slightest interest for me.'

'How can you be so sure when you haven't heard it?' he asked mildly. He stopped where there was a parking space and turned in his seat to look at her. 'You're behaving like a sulky child, Imogen. I thought you had more sophistication. Why don't you try to be your age?'

A suggestion which did nothing to sweeten her. With her eyes fixed upon the instruments on the dashboard, she said coldly:

'Frankly, after last night I dislike you, Mr Wainwright, and I don't want to spend any more time in your company than I must.'

That, she thought, was rude enough to send him hurtling homeward, but instead he laughed outright.

'Really venomous, aren't you? Those green eyes of yours are glittering like a snake's. Would you really like to poison me, Imogen?'

She looked up into his mocking eyes fiercely.

'I should enjoy seeing you writhe!'

'You wouldn't, you know, it would be a most unpleasant sight. But about that cup of tea—I'm certain you're longing for one, and you're being very foolish to deny yourself for the pleasure of snubbing me.' He got out of the car and came round to open her door. 'Come along, and don't be an idiot.'

She met his gaze and then she too laughed. He was right, she had been behaving childishly. That was not the way in which Vivien would have handled the situation; she would have obtained her cup of tea at the price of some insincere pleasantries. Nor would she have baulked at a kiss or two—after all, what was there in a kiss?

'I think you're unsnubbable,' she told him. 'But if you're ready to forgive my rudeness, I'll come.' She got out of the car. 'Where do we go?'

'Down here.'

Disconcertingly he took hold of her elbow to guide her over the road. The contact agitated her nerves, much to her annoyance. She wanted to be wholly indifferent to him, but her body played her false. Our chemistry must be complementary, she told herself, striving by the clinical explanation to neutralise the effect proximity to this man always had upon her.

Seeking to distract herself, she looked about her. To their left was the arcaded crescent, and the green hill above Saint Ann's Well, but he led her away from it into the main street which led towards the Dales with the railway viaduct at its end.

'Seems quite a busy town,' she remarked, trying to sound casual, and wished he would remove his hand from her arm. She noticed how every woman they passed looked at him.

'In the season it's a very busy place, but that hasn't begun yet. It was famous for its spa even in Roman times. People of more recent date used to come here to take the baths, but nowadays the efficaciousness of spa water has been exploded. It's a good centre for tourists.' He stopped outside a café. 'I think this will do.'

He released her elbow to allow her to precede him into it.

He chatted on about the country while they were served. The road to the south led to Miller's Dale, Chee Dale and other famous spots. Westwards was the climb up to the moors, and the Cat and Fiddle, second highest pub in England. But when the waitress had brought the tea and cakes which he had ordered, he stopped and looked at her searchingly.

'With reference to this proposition about which you were so rude, if you can tear yourself away from Terpsichore for a few months, how would you like to visit a foreign country?'

Startled, she exclaimed: 'I've always wanted to travel.'

'This would be an opportunity. I know Sweden isn't as romantic as the Mediterranean countries, but parts of it are very beautiful—immense lakes, immense forests. It's a very clean and efficiently run country.'

She recollected that he was half Swedish himself. It was his other country which he was describing, but why ever did he want her to go there? She voiced her query.

'It's to help my sister Greta,' he explained. 'She's on a farm in mid-Sweden, which belonged to her husband, who, you may have gathered, met with a fatal accident. She wants to dispose of the property and move south to Stockholm, where she has found a flat, and where she can resume her old job of teaching. There are two young children, and she wants someone whom she can trust to take charge of them, both during the move and possibly afterwards. She is very lonely, Imogen, and has not been very well. Not only she herself, but Letty and Father would be immensely grateful if you would step into the breach. You will of course receive a salary, and it would be quite an adventure for you.'

He looked at her almost appealingly.

'I'm sure it would,' Imogen said a little drily. 'But I'm not domesticated. Besides, wouldn't she prefer a Swedish girl?'

'She particularly wants an English one. She finds Swedish women too independent. Don't forget she's half English herself. She asked me to find out if Letty knew anyone who would like a few months abroad.'

'And so you discussed it among yourselves and decided I was a possibility?' She was not flattered, in fact she could have laughed, in spite of her vexation, for the situation was so ironic. All her efforts to appear as an ultra-modern girl, only out for kicks, seemed to have misfired badly. Peter persisted in regarding her as a nice girl, with a warm heart concealed beneath her sophistication, while Christian, who had called her a witch and a tiger cat, which seemed more promising, had been merely probing her to discover her potentialities as a mother's help! Lettice must have told him she was out of a job and might be available.

Nobody would ever consider Vivien in such a category, she thought wryly, but she herself had neither the looks nor the detachment to be a successful femme fatale.

'Knowing your opinion of me,' she went on, 'I'm surprised that you want to foist me on to your sister.'

'Are you so sure you know my opinion of you?' he asked with an odd smile.

'I seem to remember you called me a bitch.'

'You wouldn't have much opportunity for bitchiness in Jamtland,' he told her, 'and your love life is your own concern. Letty declares that you're reliable and conscientious, and I've also made my own observations.'

'Have you really?' She was annoyed. 'You seem to have dissected me pretty thoroughly. But you know I'm a dancer, not a slavey. What makes you think I would be suitable?'

'Your way with children. I've watched you with Teddy and Pam. I can see you're fond of them and you understand them. Poor little Sven and Kajsa have had a thin time. Their father was a bit of a martinet, he believed that children should be seen and not heard, and Greta, like many Swedish mothers, always seems so detached. Not that I'm blaming her,' he put in hastily, 'she has so much else to do, she has little time for them. I'm sorry for those kids, Imogen, and I'm sure you could do a lot to help them if you would.'

She was immensely surprised. She had not thought Christian was the type of man to be concerned about children's welfare, but she knew he was fond of his small half-brother and sister, who were definitely heard as well as seen.

Looking at him curiously, she said:

'So you're trying to appeal to my better nature and my maternal instincts? I don't think I've got either.'

As a sophisticated modern go-getter, she could not admit to such weaknesses.

'Come off it, Imogen!' He smiled at her winningly.

'You're not all that bad.'

'Thanks very much.' She was sarcastic. 'And if I accept this—er—position, what's the drill?'

'I'm going up to Jamtland for the Åre Sports Week at the beginning of March. Western Jamtland adjoins the Norwegian border and Åre is not only a tourist centre in summer, but it's favoured by winter sportsmen. I thought of founding my school there, but it is a little remote. I've a sentimental feeling for the place because it was on Mount Areskutan that I first learned to ski. I would take you with me and leave you with Greta while I went on to Åre.'

'The beginning of March! But we're nearly at the end of February now. That doesn't give much time.'

'Do you need time to decide?'

'Of course I do. I have to go back to London and see about the flat and all sorts of things. You may be able to rush off to the other ends of the earth at a moment's notice, but I have commitments.'

'So I can add to your virtues a sense of responsibility?'

She flushed as if she had admitted to a crime. It would be rather fun to rush off to Sweden with Christian, but she did not think it would be very wise; he might be indifferent, but her own feelings towards him were mixed. She was both antagonised and attracted by him, and if she saw too much of him, the attraction might win. She said firmly:

'I'd better say no at once, so you can find someone else.' But she was aware of regret.

'If you turn it down, I shan't bother,' he said casually, 'Greta will have to manage with a local girl.'

'I suppose I'm your second failure,' she said thoughtfully. 'Did Miss Brayshaw turn it down too?'

'Erica?' He raised his brows. 'I haven't approached her.'

'Why not? I should have thought she would have

been the first person to occur to you.'

'She did,' he agreed, 'but upon reflection, I decided not. Unlike yourself I'm scrupulous about arousing false hopes. To install her with my sister might put ideas into her head. I'd hate her to think it was the first step towards a declaration.'

Recalling what Peter had said about the erotic effect upon him of moonlight and pretty girls, she asked reproachfully:

'So you led her on, and now want to be rid of her?'

'She didn't need any leading,' he said sardonically. 'Believe me, I'm no Casanova. It's as much for her sake as for mine that I don't want to encourage any illusions.'

'And you're sure I haven't got any?' Her lips curved mischievously.

'About me?' He grinned. 'You've made that plain, haven't you? You'll be under no misapprehensions.'

Her eyes glinting like green jewels, for she was enjoying herself, Imogen looked arch.

'Are you quite sure about that?' she murmured.

'As sure as I can be about anything female. You've said you don't like me, and you didn't respond to my —er—overtures.'

'So when you—when you kissed me, you were testing me?' she asked indignantly.

'Perhaps.' His eyes mocked her.

'You cold-blooded brute!' The words slipped out before she could check them.

He began to laugh. 'Your reaction was most satisfactory.'

'Oh!' She clenched her fists under the tablecloth. She would have liked to have smacked his face again.

'In one thing you are perfectly correct,' she went on tersely. 'I do dislike you, and if your sister resembles you...'

'She couldn't,' he interrupted her. 'What you dislike about me is the fact that I'm a man and not one whom you can twist round your fingers. But once I've taken you there, you won't be seeing me. After Åre, I'll be going to Spain with the World Cup team.'

She checked an angry riposte. There was no point in bandying further words with him, and his indifference was satisfactory—or was it?

She asked curiously: 'Have you decided never to marry?'

'No, but it's one of the things that will have to wait until I retire from racing. I couldn't expect any woman to put up with my continual absences. I have to follow the snow for my training. When it has gone from Europe, there's always the Andes. The last Olympic team trained in Chile throughout the summer.'

'Skiing is your whole life, isn't it?' she asked a little wistfully. She had wanted to make dancing hers, but had not had the opportunities. As for Christian, he could do without women so long as he could find snow.

'You could say so,' he agreed.

'Tell me about it,' she urged, aware of a desire to share his interest. 'I'm very ignorant about it all. What happens when you race?'

'There are various events—cross-country, ski-jumping, the downhill and the slalom. It's the last two that are my specialities. The downhill is, as it suggests, a vertical descent, over courses varying from two thousand to seven thousand feet. There are control gates through which one has to pass, sometimes turns among trees—tricky, that, but on a straight chute I've reached a speed of ninety miles an hour. It's a marvellous sensation, the nearest man can get to flying, much more so than sitting in a plane.'

Enthusiasm lit up his eyes with blue flame. He was not seeing her at all but the white hillside, savouring the memory of that fantastic speed. His passion for racing was greater far than any woman could arouse.

'Then there is the slalom,' he went on. 'This is much slower. A slalom course can have as many as seventy-three gates, over a prepared course of from four hundred to six hundred feet. A gate is two poles with flags, about ten feet apart through which the skier has to pass. In a slalom race one does two runs, the gates being altered for the second one. It entails dozens of turns which only a feeling for the course, a sort of harmony with it, can unravel. One mustn't charge through too fast, each turn should be in a smooth arc, so that the movement is never broken, never halted ... but you've probably seen it all on television.'

She did not like to confess that she did not like watching sports programmes, but he did not seem to expect any answer. His whole face was lit up, with a kind of glow. Involuntarily she thought how irresistible he would be if love could light that fire in him, and quickly dismissed the thought from her mind. Christian's potential lovemaking was not a subject she wanted to dwell upon. It was too disturbing.

'I thought that once I had won a gold medal, I should be satisfied,' he concluded, 'but now I want a second one. That's human nature.' He smiled almost apologetically.

'I hope you get it,' she said carelessly. 'But regarding your sister, I think not. I share a flat in London with two friends and I don't want to give it up until I'm quite sure I can't get work in my own line.'

'Think it over,' he urged her. 'Talk it over with Letty.'

This Imogen had no intention of doing, she had made up her mind, but Lettice herself brought up the subject.

They were in the kitchen washing up the tea things. Most confidential conversations at Barley Howe took place in that room. It was rarely that the sitting-room did not contain either the children or the menfolk.

'I wish you'd go, Imo,' Lettice said. 'Joe's worried about Greta. After all, she is his daughter. She's had a bit of trouble and she's half Swedish. You know how broody Swedes can get, and the suicide rate is so high —something to do with those interminable dark winters. You're just the sort of person who would cheer her up.'

Imogen gave her reasons for refusing, though Lettice's plea had shaken her. The Wainwrights had been very kind to her and she would like to oblige them.

'Frankly, Letty,' she concluded, 'I don't get on awfully well with Christian.'

'But you won't be seeing him after the start, and the children do need someone like you.' She looked at Imogen appealingly. 'It isn't Pete who's keeping you back?'

'Good heavens, no, Letty. I don't want to get entangled with any man ever again. You see, I was let down, that's partly why I got into such a bad state. I came up here to forget.'

But even while she spoke, she realised with surprise how greatly the pain of her loss had lessened. In the short time that she had been in Derbyshire, Raymond had receded so far away that she could only recall him with a conscious effort. She supposed all the new impressions she had received had crowded him out of her thoughts, but she feared that London would bring him back again, being so full of associations with him. She almost hoped it would, she did not like to think that she could forget so easily.

'Oh, you poor kid!' Lettice turned from the sink where she was washing up with her eyes full of sympathy.

'I've finished with men,' Imogen announced dramatically.

'But, darling, you can't judge the whole sex by one

81

rotter,' Lettice pointed out. 'You've been unlucky, but you'll get over it and find someone who won't let you down.'

'I'd never be certain of that,' Imogen said bitterly. 'Once bitten, twice shy.'

'But I'm sure neither Peter nor Christian...'

'They won't get the chance,' Imogen interrupted. 'And you're wrong about Christian, he's just the type to take his fun and ride away.'

'I think you wrong him,' Lettice told her. 'But it's Greta you'll be living with, not Christian, and she, poor girl, has had husband trouble before Sven died, so you'll be able to indulge your man-hating together. Not that you'll keep it up, it isn't natural. I don't mind betting you'll find yourself wed before another year has passed.'

'If I were a gambler, which I'm not, I'd take you up on that,' Imogen laughed. 'And as regards Sweden, if on my return, there's nothing doing, I might go there, if the girls can find another flatmate.'

A letter from Vivien next day disposed of that problem. Her show, she wrote, was folding, had been playing to empty houses, but she had managed to secure a good part in a touring company for the spring and summer. Louise was getting married, possibly was already married.

'She was a bit elusive about it,' Vivien wrote in her breezy style, 'because there's an urgent reason for it. Who would have thought it of our ultra-respectable Lou? The point is that she and Godfrey desperately need somewhere to live, or else she wouldn't have told me, for of course she's after this flat. I told her she must settle that with you, you had as much right to the place as she has—more, in fact, since the tenancy is in your name by virtue of your father's guarantee. What will you do? Transfer it to her, or look for other flatmates? You'd better come back and sort things out.'

Imogen's reaction was principally annoyance with Louise for her lack of prudence; the situation had become too common to shock her. It looked as if she would have to surrender the flat to the newlyweds. She had been happy with Vivien and Louise, but she was disinclined to seek for two strange girls to share with her. Fate seemed to be conspiring to send her to Sweden.

She rang up her agent, but he had nothing definite to offer her. That was not conclusive, she knew that he gave preference to clients on the spot and she had told him she needed a holiday. It was just possible something might turn up at the last moment, but not likely.

She explained the position frankly to Lettice, and told her that if nothing did, she would be pleased to accept the position with Greta, unless they found someone more suitable in the meantime.

'That's improbable,' Lettice told her. 'Christian is determined that you and none other shall go to Greta's rescue.'

'But my profession comes first,' Imogen insisted, wondering just why Christian was so keen about engaging her.

It crossed her mind that the skiing lesson had been in the nature of an endurance test. Mid-Sweden in early spring would not be a bed of roses, and he had no wish to saddle his sister with a girl who wept when circumstances were too much for her. He might enjoy drying feminine tears, since such weakness would flatter his masculine ego, but Greta required someone with stamina.

Such a supposition was hardly flattering to herself, neither did it do anything towards endearing Christian to her, but she felt it was a challenge. She feared neither winter weather nor hard work, and she would like to show Christian that she was equal to them.

Lettice, who was watching her shrewdly, said:

'I can't help wishing that you don't get anything else. After all, you can always go back to dancing when you've had enough of Sweden, and if you're still there next summer, we'll be coming out to join you for our holidays.'

'That would be nice,' Imogen agreed, but in the cutting wind which was blowing round Castleton, summer seemed a long way ahead. 'Meanwhile I must return to London at once.'

However, it was late to start that day, when she had not even packed, so she decided to leave early the next morning.

When Christian heard of her decision, he offered to drive her down, as he also was going to London.

'It's quicker and pleasanter than travelling by train,' he pointed out.

'Thank you, but no,' she said hastily. She shrank from the prospect of a long tête-à-tête with him. She would have quite enough of him if she went with him to Sweden, but that had not yet been decided. In any case, in an aeroplane, there would be many other passengers.

'Why waste money on your rail fare?' he asked practically. And as if suspecting her thoughts, he added:

'We shan't be alone. I'm giving the Brayshaws a lift. Erica and her brother are going to spend a week in London, so you may as well join the party.'

That altered the situation, and as she had so far not met Erica she was curious to see her. So she accepted his offer, thanking him with better grace than she had previously shown.

That afternoon Peter was brought home from the hospital. The ambulance pulled up next door, much to the children's excitement. They dashed out into the garden to watch the proceedings before Imogen could stop them. She did not go after them, for she felt sure

that Peter would not want her to witness his undig-
nified descent from the vehicle.

They came in again, after a sharp rebuff from Mrs
Lethwaite.

'He'd got two wooden legs,' Pamela announced,
round eyed.

'Those were crutches, silly,' Teddy told her with
superiority. 'They're to hold him up.' He looked at
Imogen anxiously. 'Will Peter always have to go about
like that?'

'Of course not. It's only until his leg is better.'

Though she had not seen it, she could visualise the
scene—Peter toiling up the garden path with the help
of the attendant. Her heart was wrung with sudden
pity for the young man who had skied so gaily about
Rushup Edge such a short while previously. It would
be a long time before he could ski again, however
quickly the break healed.

Thus it was that she went over to welcome him
home that evening in a softened mood. She found him
fully dressed, but lying on a divan which had been
brought into the Lethwaites' front room, so that he
would not have to go upstairs. A rug was flung over his
legs concealing the plaster.

Mrs Lethwaite ushered her in, saying how glad she
was to see her, as Peter seemed terribly depressed.

He put down the book he was reading, and made an
instinctive effort to rise, and she ran to him to prevent
him.

'Don't try to move.'

He sank back on the cushions supporting him with a
twisted smile.

'It's an awful effort.'

She dropped on her knees beside him, feeling more
moved than she had done in the hospital. It seemed
infinitely worse finding him crippled among his own
surroundings, than in a hospital bed, it brought home

his helplessness to her.

'It's sad to see you like this,' she said gently. 'I'm so sorry, Peter.'

'So am I, and six weeks seems an interminable time. I shan't even have you to cheer me. Christian's been in. He says you're going back to London. Why, Imogen? Couldn't you wait until I'm better?'

'I wish I could,' she said untruthfully. With Peter in this state she might become involved much more deeply than she wished. Somewhere someone had said pity was akin to love. But she was glad Christian had broken the news of her departure and she had not got to tell him herself.

She explained her reasons for going, hoping Christian had not mentioned the Swedish project, for she was sure Peter would read a false significance into that. Apparently he had not, for they talked about London and her prospects of getting a job.

'I hope you'll be in another television series soon, and then I can watch you,' he told her.

'I'd like that too, it was fun,' but that again was a half truth. Such an engagement would be too full of memories of Raymond.

He dropped a hand to stroke her hair, and she made no move to stop him. Let him have what comfort he could gain from her presence. The firelight flickered on her white sweater. She was all in white, wearing white corded trousers. Only the light beside the divan was on, its radiance dimmed by an amber shade. The scene was cosy and intimate.

'I'll never forget you, Imogen,' he said earnestly, 'though I don't think you've much use for me.'

'Don't say that, Pete.' She lifted her head and met the sentimental gaze of his brown eyes, wishing he did not remind her of a spaniel her father had once owned. Misplaced affection was such a waste, she thought bitterly. Hers for Raymond, Peter's for her—

there ought to be a better way of arranging such matters.

'You're my friend,' she told him, 'and I never forget my friends.'

'Ah, friend,' he said a little scornfully, then smiled repentantly. 'I mustn't be greedy. You'll write and tell me how you get on?'

'If you want me to.' She was reluctant to do so.

'Don't if it's a bore...' he told her quickly.

'Oh, it wouldn't be that.' But if she went to Sweden he would learn her movements from the stamps, and blame her for duplicity, but she was not going to risk a jealous storm over Christian for which there was no grounds.

She made an effort to be bright and amusing, talking about the children, her home, her work, anything except Christian, and after that first remark of his, neither spoke his name again. Yet he was there, in both their thoughts—Peter's because he imagined she had a yen for him, while Imogen could visualise his satirical smile, imagine his words:

'What do you think you're doing now, if you're not playing him up?'

But she was only being sympathetic, and how could she be otherwise?

When she said she must go, as she had her packing to do, Peter asked:

'Will you kiss me goodbye? Just this once.'

It was a very chaste salute, a mere touching of lips, but he seemed satisfied.

As she went down the passage, she saw Mrs Lethwaite was admitting a girl whom she recognised as the nurse who had tended Peter in the hospital. It transpired that the girl had relations in Castleton whom she visited upon her off days, and she had called in upon her way back to enquire about her ex-patient.

'Just to see he's suffering no ill effects from the journey over here,' she was saying shyly to Mrs Lethwaite.

Peter's mother showed her straight into the room which Imogen had just vacated, and as she opened the front door, Imogen heard the note of glad welcome in Peter's voice. She thought with relief that it would not be long before that young man had found consolation.

Outside it was snowing a little; she hoped it would not lie and delay her start upon the morrow. Snow had been her principal impression of Derbyshire. She ran down the garden path and up the one to Barley Howe, for she had no coat, and arrived breathless in the hall. Christian turned from the telephone, having completed a call, as she came in, and stood barring her way. He surveyed her white-clad figure, with what seemed to her to be a supercilious air.

'Been taking a tender farewell?' he asked with a jeering note in his voice, 'but you seem in a mighty hurry to get away from him.'

His expression jarred upon Imogen, for she had been affected by the scene which she had gone through, and she said sharply:

'I ran because I hadn't a coat, and I'm terribly sorry for poor Peter.'

'Really?' He was sardonic.

'Yes, really,' she said hotly. 'I'm not heartless...' and checked herself, aghast. She had betrayed herself completely, forgetting that she had represented herself to both young men as being without feeling.

'I'm very glad to hear it,' he said sincerely. 'Why then do you always try to make out you're so hard-boiled? You're really quite a nice girl.'

The description stung. 'Nice girl' sounded so terribly banal. That all her efforts should culminate in being considered anything so ordinary was humiliating.

'If you think that,' she told him disdainfully, 'you're in for a big surprise!'

He raised his brows, and his eyes twinkled.

'I don't think you can surprise me, Imogen,' he remarked.

'Wait and see,' she retorted, 'and if you'll kindly let me pass, I've some packing to do.'

He stood aside and she passed him with heightened colour. At the foot of the stairs, she turned back to say:

'You'll find I can be perfectly horrible when I choose.'

'That will have to be experienced to be believed,' he declared.

She ran lightly up the stairs, pursued by his laughter.

The snow had vanished by morning, and it was a day of sunshine and light showers when Imogen took her leave of Barley Howe. Cloud shadows raced over the brown and green slopes of the hills. The trees were still leafless, and there were few hedges, unmortared stone walls divided the fields.

Lettice and Joseph bade her an affectionate farewell, with many invitations to come again, and reiterated their hope that she would go to Sweden and that they would meet there again in the summer.

The children had been desolate to learn of her departure. They had become great friends and she was an unfailing source of bedtime stories. She gave each of them a silver penny, fifty pence, which was received with avidity, and they were so busy discussing what they would buy with her bounty that they had no time to bewail her departure.

She wore the same green woollen dress which she had been wearing upon her arrival, and her camel travelling coat. Since she was returning to city life she had made up her eyes and lips. She saw Christian look at her with a twist of his flexible mouth, while he murmured:

'Miss Sinclair has resumed her sophistication!'

He looked unfamiliar in a dark suit and a suede car coat, since hitherto she had always seen him in informal sports clothes. He was in a hurry to be off and bundled her without ceremony into the front seat of his estate car, while Joe stowed her cases in the back. From the window of the Lethwaites' house, Peter waved to her.

Then they were off, sliding down the slope towards Hope, to pick up the Brayshaws, who lived there.

'And I hope to goodness they don't keep us waiting,' Christian observed.

'Are they unpunctual, then?'

'Oh, you know what girls are when they're dressing up. They have no sense of time.'

'I have.'

He shot her an amused glance. 'That has yet to be proved.'

Barley Howe was left behind. Imogen realised that she was leaving it in a much more sanguine state of mind than that in which she had arrived. Her cure had been partly accomplished. What lay ahead was intriguing. Either her agent would have turned up something worth while for her, or else she would be going to an unknown country. Either possibility was exciting.

CHAPTER FIVE

GEORGE BRAYSHAW was waiting for them beside a couple of suitcases when they drove up to the front door of the Brayshaws' modern bungalow.

'Erica won't be a minute,' he said as he stowed his luggage in the car.

Christian looked significantly at his watch and winked at Imogen. 'Late as usual,' he said.

Five minutes passed, and then he impatiently sounded his horn.

The summons brought Erica out, though she did not hurry, and Imogen looked at her curiously.

There was nothing very outstanding about her. Like her brother, she had brown hair and brown eyes. She was very small and dainty, but the red trouser suit she was wearing was ill-chosen, her legs were too short for trousers, and her petite prettiness cried out for more feminine attire. She was so heavily made up that Imogen thought she looked like a doll.

George, who had taken his seat in the back of the car, opened the door for her, but Erica hesitated, throwing an appealing glance at Christian. All he said was:

'Hurry up and get in, we've a long way to go!'

She climbed in reluctantly, looking sulky, and knowing that she had expected to sit beside Christian, Imogen asked:

'Wouldn't Miss Brayshaw like to sit in front?' wishing that she had suggested the move while they were waiting.

'She's all right where she is,' he returned, and put the car in gear.

He drove down to Chesterfield, famed for its crooked church spire, a town set among open moorland country.

The crooked spire excited Imogen's interest. The herringbone pattern of the lead covering on each upward facet of the spire accentuated the twist. George assured her that it was quite stable and put forward some of the various theories suggested for its crookedness, but Christian insisted that it was merely an unsuccessful early experiment in constructing a perpendicular spiral of wood covered with lead.

Beyond Chesterfield, the hills were left behind, as they turned on to the motorway leading south.

'No more scenery,' Christian told Imogen. 'Motorways are the quickest way of getting from A to Z, but they're all deadly monotonous.'

Which was only too true. A double line of concrete separated by a green lane—banks upon either side, crossed by identical bridges—mile after mile, with the swish of passing cars a vaguely sinister accompaniment to their progress.

George chatted amiably with the two in front, but Erica was silent. Imogen suspected that she was still sulking. Neither did Christian address any remark to her directly. She was sitting behind him, and once or twice, Imogen saw him glance at the driving mirror in which he could no doubt see her reflection with an ironical smile on his lips. He was perfectly aware of the reason for Erica's displeasure, and had deliberately engineered it. The girl was lacking in pride, Imogen decided. Had she been in her place, not for worlds would she have betrayed how his neglect had annoyed her. As it was, he was simply amused by her attitude.

George began to mutter about lunch and Erica showed some signs of animation.

'You must need a rest, Christian,' she urged. 'You've driven over a hundred miles and all the worst part going into London is still to come.'

'If you're hungry, why don't you say so?' he asked her irritably. 'I could do the whole distance without a break, and still be equal to tackling the London traffic. What about you, Imogen, would you like to stop?'

'I wouldn't mind a halt,' she admitted.

'There's no desperate hurry, surely?' George supported her.

'Not really, only some business that I'm anxious to get settled as soon as possible.'

He ventured to shoot Imogen a barbed glance, and hastily returned it to the road. Imogen smiled to herself. If he thought she was going to hustle through her own affairs to suit him, he was going to be disappointed!

He obligingly turned off the M1 and drove into a Midland town. There was the usual difficulty of finding a place to park within reasonable distance of the town centre, but eventually that was accomplished and they left the car. Erica immediately took possession of Christian, slipping her hand through his arm, though she had to almost skip along to keep pace with his long strides, which he did not modify to accommodate her. Imogen noticed that she was wearing absurd high-heeled sandals which looked quite wrong with her suit. She was beginning to understand what Christian had meant when he had said Erica needed no encouragement. She followed them with George.

'You didn't stay long with the Wainwrights,' he remarked. 'I thought you'd be there until Easter.'

'I don't know what gave you that idea,' she said. 'I'm a working girl, you know, not a lady of leisure, and it's time I got back into harness.'

He looked at her with interest. 'You're on the stage, aren't you?'

'When I can get a shop. It's an overcrowded profession.' She did not mention Sweden.

93

Over the roast beef and Yorkshire pudding which was the main dish on the menu, Erica remarked petulantly:

'I hear there's actually been skiing on Rushup Edge, and you gave quite an exhibition, Christian. Of course you would come the weekend I was away. You might have phoned me.'

A speech which was revealing. Evidently this was the first time that she had seen Christian since her return. The arrangements for the journey had been made through George.

'I did, but you'd gone to Buxton,' Christian reminded her.

'The Bennetts are on the phone. If you'd rung me, I'd have come back.'

'I didn't want to spoil your weekend, and I'm sure your friends would never have forgiven me for taking you away.'

'You know I'd rather have been with you.'

He smiled a little derisively. 'Could you explain that to the Bennetts?'

'Of course she couldn't,' George said heartily. 'They wouldn't understand her infatuation for you.'

Erica flushed. 'George, you're a pig,' she told him. 'Christian promised to teach me to ski, and it isn't often that we can at Castleton. It was an opportunity which may never come again.'

'Christian made the most of it,' George said tactlessly, 'he found another pupil.'

Local gossip had reported all Christian's actions.

Erica gave Imogen a glance like vitriol. 'So I heard.'

'The lesson wasn't a success,' Imogen hastened to inform her. 'I'd much rather you had had it instead of me.'

Would Christian have let this dainty little person toil up that slope carrying her skis? She was certain he would not have done so, but for all that he did not seem to be very enthralled with Erica. Possibly he was already tired of her.

In the powder room, while the two girls were repairing their make-up, Erica said spitefully:

'I suppose you've fallen for Christian, but you realise he'll never reciprocate?'

'I've no personal interest in Mr Wainwright whatever,' Imogen assured her. 'I just happened to be there and it amused him to make fun of my efforts.'

Erica looked surprised by this information.

'He's my boy,' she stated emphatically. 'So long as you understand that.'

Imogen thought that Christian had his own ideas upon that point, and felt sorry for Erica. It was a bold girl who dared to lay claim to Christian, who was obsessed by his skiing. She knew he planned to go to Sweden, Spain, and after that South America, and it would be a very long time before he saw Erica again. She suspected Erica's possessive assumption was a piece of bravado, designed to warn her off, but he must have given her some grounds for making it. Men were all alike, deceivers ever.

'I always understood he was your friend,' she said tactfully, 'and I've no wish whatever to butt in.'

With this assurance, Erica became all candid friendliness, displaying a kittenish charm.

'Then that's all right,' she said happily. 'I thought it was as well to make the situation clear. I shall be in London for several days to shop for the summer, and I expect he'll take me to some shows. I wonder ... could you take George off our hands?'

But Imogen jibbed at that suggestion. If George knew the position, surely he could be trusted to find his own diversions? Erica shrugged and pouted.

'I daresay, but he likes you, I thought it would be the obvious solution.'

Imogen insisted that she had too much else to do.

She had no wish to entangle with George and perhaps have Christian taking up the cudgels on his behalf. His opinion of her in that respect was quite low enough without adding to it.

They arrived in the afternoon just before the evening rush, and even so were subject to the usual traffic blocks and slow progress through congested traffic. Imogen had to admire Christian's skilful driving. He dropped the Brayshaws at their Bloomsbury hotel, but scouted Imogen's suggestion that he should leave her to make her way from there.

'What about your luggage?'

'I could get a taxi.'

'Quite unnecessary. Tell me where to go.'

Under her direction they arrived at the flat.

He insisted upon carrying up her cases to the top floor, so she had no option but to ask him to come in.

Vivien in a glamorous negligée was lolling on the divan in the sitting-room. She sprang up as they appeared.

'Hi, kiddo! You're looking better. Who is this?'

Imogen introduced them.

'Excuse my get-up,' Vivien said easily to Christian. 'I was resting.'

She was studying him with undisguised interest. Vivien was looking very beautiful, the rich colours of her robe enhancing her big, dark eyes and dense black hair. Her almost oriental loveliness contrasted with his Nordic fairness. Imogen thought that from the aesthetic point of view, she had never seen a better matched couple.

'I'm sorry I disturbed you,' he said politely, and smiled. 'The get-up is most fetching.'

'Liberty's,' she told him. 'They favour the exotic and so do I. I'm very glad you've come, I was feeling bored. Can I offer you anything? We've only tea or coffee, I'm afraid.'

Christian said that he must go. He turned to Imogen and to her surprise, asked if she would join him and the Brayshaws for dinner. She surmised that, like Erica, he wanted her to come and amuse George. Again she made excuses, aware that Vivien's arched brows had risen.

'If you can't, that's it,' he said indifferently, and looked at Vivien. 'I suppose you wouldn't take pity on us and make up a foursome?'

'I'd be delighted—that is, if Imo is sure she doesn't want to go.'

'Imogen's had enough of my society for one day,' Christian said, laughing, and proceeded to make arrangements to meet her friend. When he had gone, Vivien looked at Imogen enquiringly.

'What a dish! If that's a sample of what they produce in Derbyshire, I can't wait to get there. But why on earth wouldn't you go, Imo? There's nothing much to eat here except baked beans.'

'Then I'm glad you're going to have a decent meal,' Imogen told her. 'But I'm afraid Mr Christian Wainwright is rather heavily involved with the female half of the other couple. You're wanted for the brother.'

'Who evidently doesn't appeal to you,' Vivien remarked shrewdly. 'But I'm only going for the food, though I don't think it would be difficult to annex your Christian if I wanted to, he's got a roving eye.'

'Well, you're an eyeful,' Imogen said, laughing, thinking poor Erica could not compete with her friend. She was fairly certain Christian was not nearly as deeply involved with Miss Brayshaw as Erica had made out. She was sorry for the other girl, but thought she might be saved some heartbreak if she discovered Christian's true colours before it was too late. Vivien, she well knew, was in no danger, and she had already assessed him correctly.

While she unpacked, storing her belongings in her share of the chest and wardrobe in the girls' room, the memories that she had feared came thronging back. Vivien was having a bath, and the little flat seemed very quiet. Raymond's image came out to her from the shadows. She could see him sitting on her divan as he had sat so often during the informal parties they had given upon Sunday nights, playing and singing to his guitar. He had always been the leading spirit of the gathering. Often they had danced to the radiogram as if they did not have enough dancing during the week. Some of his essence still lingered about the place, so perhaps it was as well that she was leaving it. It did her no good to be constantly reminded of him, when she was as sundered from him as if he had never existed.

Vivien dressed herself in a black cocktail gown—the proverbial little black dress—and she looked lovely and glowing. Imogen wondered a little maliciously how Erica would react to this addition to the party.

She felt depressed when Vivien had left, but attributed her mood to fatigue. She could not possibly be regretting her refusal of Christian's invitation.

Louise came in from her office, and was grateful for the meal Imogen had cooked—an omelette with tinned mushrooms. Almost her first question was what had Imogen decided about the flat?

'You can have it transferred to you, or rather Godfrey,' Imogen told her. 'I shan't stay on here whatever I decide to do.'

'But are you quite certain?' Louise began. 'I mean, we don't want to turn you out ... though it would be an enormous relief to be sure of a roof over our heads.'

'Yes. I don't want to stay here, too many memories,' Imogen assured her. 'I haven't congratulated you, Lou, when's the ceremony?'

Louise looked a little shamefaced. 'It was last week,

actually, in a register office. You see, we thought the sooner the better.'

'Of course.' She kissed Louise's embarrassed face. 'I'm not blaming you, love, and I hope you'll be very happy.'

'Oh, we will. I've always wanted a baby. I'll go and tell Godfrey about the flat as soon as I've helped you wash up. He's been marvellous.'

Imogen smiled wryly. Godfrey was as much responsible for the situation as Louise was and he was only behaving as he ought to do, but she said nothing. If Louise liked to think he was marvellous, so much the better—for Godfrey.

When Louise went rushing off to meet her husband, Imogen's sense of isolation increased. It was not much of a homecoming to be left on her own. She was just about to prepare the divan for its nocturnal function when Vivien's key turned in the lock. She came in, sparkling and vivacious, followed, to Imogen's astonishment, by Christian. He was carrying a cardboard carton and some bottles.

'Christian decided to come back with me and cheer you up,' Vivien announced gaily. 'You haven't had much of a welcome up to now. Where's Lou?'

As if on cue, Louise came in.

'Godfrey's ever so grateful,' she began, then seeing the visitor. 'Oh!'

Imogen hastened to introduce them. Louise looked selfconscious and batted her sandy eyelashes. She found Christian a little overwhelming.

'Sit down, Christian.' Vivien indicated the divan. 'I'll get some glasses.' She looked at the other two impishly. 'Christian wanted to know how three females can manage to live together in harmony, so I asked him to come and see. Lou, take that carton into the kitchen.' She was, as she spoke, putting wine glasses on the table. 'I'll come and help you unpack it. Christian, here's the corkscrew.'

The bottles contained champagne.

As her flatmates went into the kitchen, Imogen looked accusingly at Christian, who was busy opening a bottle.

'What have you done with the Brayshaws?' she asked.

'Nothing. I hope they're safely tucked up in their beds,' he returned. 'I took them to their hotel and then came on here with Vivien. I didn't realise you lived with a raving beauty.'

'Should I have told you so?'

'By no means. It would have spoilt the enchanting surprise.'

The cork came out with a loud plop. 'Quick—the glasses! We don't want to waste all the fizz.'

It transpired that they had raided a late serving delicatessen shop in Soho and the food Vivien produced was somewhat surprising. There was ravioli, which she had heated, strange kinds of sausage, potato and mixed salads.

The champagne loosened their tongues, and Louise became giggly. Vivien sprawled on the divan with her arm round Christian's neck, making outrageous remarks, which he capped by even more audacious suggestions, while Louise giggled appreciatively. Only Imogen could not join wholeheartedly in their nonsense. It was like old times, but with a difference. Raymond should have been there. She ascribed her lack of enthusiasm to his absence, though it was not wholly so. Louise, who must have received some thought-transference, remarked suddenly:

'If only Ray were here, he'd have given us some music.' She was still unaware that Raymond had broken with Imogen.

'Ray? Who's he?' Christian asked, suddenly alert.

'He's Imo's boy-friend, and he's on tour in Australia.'

Christian looked at Imogen. 'I hadn't heard about that one.'

'Oh, he's a back number,' she returned, flushing.

'In that case there's no need for the soulful look.' He reached up and pulled her down beside him on the divan between himself and the wall. 'Sorry there's no room for you,' he said to Louise. 'The harem's full.'

Louise giggled again.

Imogen wanted to tear herself away, but Christian's arm was close about her, clamping her to his side, and she was crushed between him and the wall. His fair hair was tousled, his eyes agleam with mischief.

Vivien on his other side, said lazily:

'With which of his slaves does my lord desire to spend the night?'

'That's hard to say.' Christian appeared to be pondering. 'I'm spoilt for choice. You, beautiful, are obviously my queen, but this one,' he squeezed Imogen's waist—'rouses the devil in me.'

He turned his head and she felt his lips upon her neck. Queer little thrills were running up her spine. Even Ray had never excited her so much. Trying to jerk away, she said fiercely:

'You're drunk.'

'It's the champagne,' Vivien explained airily. 'A man has a right to get drunk when he supplies the booze.'

'This is quite an orgy!' Louise exclaimed delightedly. 'Christian, have another drink?'

She refilled her own glass with a none too steady hand.

'Steady on, kid,' Vivien remonstrated. 'You've had quite enough. It isn't good for the chick.'

'The what?' Christian asked.

'My baby,' Louise said proudly. 'I'm married, you know.' She looked with pleasure at her new wedding ring.

'Well, well, surprise upon surprise!' Christian drawled. 'So she's beaten you two beauties to the altar.' He looked with interest at Louise's homely face.

'They're too particular,' Louise explained modestly, 'and Vivien's been and come back again.'

'Meaning?'

'We don't want to go into my private history,' Vivien said quickly. 'You men are all rotters.' She pulled Christian's hair.

'Not my Godfrey,' Louise defended her spouse.

'That remains to be seen,' Vivien said darkly. 'Drink up, Christian, there's quite a bit left. Let's drown our murky pasts in fizz.' She looked significantly at Imogen.

'No more, thanks,' Christian declined. 'I'm in training.'

He disengaged himself from the two girls and stood up, smoothing his hair, and reached for his discarded jacket. He was perfectly sober, belying Imogen's accusation.

'Thank you, ladies, for a delightful evening,' he said courteously. 'No, Lou, I really won't have any more,' as she pushed a glass towards him. 'I've got to drive back to my hotel.'

'Sure you're fit?' Vivien asked. 'You can always share the divan with Imogen.'

'I'd like nothing better,' he returned, 'but I'm sorry to disappoint you, Imogen, the time is not yet.'

'I'm not in the least disappointed,' she returned. 'I prefer my bed to myself.'

'How very early Victorian,' he drawled. 'You just aren't with it, are you, honey? Well, goodnight, girls.'

He kissed them all, Imogen last and full on her mouth. Vivien went with him to the door and insisted upon accompanying him downstairs. Their gay voices floated up to the other two. Louise ran to the window

102

and peered out.

'Coo, what a whale of a car! I hope he's fit to drive.'

Imogen said furiously:

'A night in a police cell would do him good. He's a public menace!' Her lips still tingled from his kiss, her body could still feel the grip of his encircling arm, while her brain fiercely rejected the tumult in her blood.

Louise turned from the window and stared at her.

'What's bitten you? I thought he was a rave.'

'So do about a dozen other girls,' Imogen said tartly, and began to collect the dirty glasses.

Louise sighed. 'Anyway, it was a bit of fun.'

Fun? Exactly. Silly lighthearted nonsense inspired by champagne. Imogen collected the remains of the food putting it on a tray and carried it into the kitchen. She put what was still edible in the fridge and started to wash up.

'Don't bother,' Vivien said from behind her. 'We can do it in the morning. My rehearsal isn't until ten.' She yawned.

'Is it a good part?'

'Excellent.' She looked keenly at her friend. 'I hear Adonis is going to escort you to Sweden. He's an improvement on the last one.'

'It isn't decided . . .' Imogen began.

'Then if the decision rests with you, clinch it. That one's worth hanging on to, and he can't possibly be serious about that little brown partridge we had dinner with.'

'He can't be serious about anyone,' Imogen insisted.

'Then you know exactly where you are with him, and he's good fun. Get all you can out of him, ducks, he's open-handed, and part without tears. Here's to *la dolce vita*!' She picked up a half full glass which was standing on the draining board, and drank it.

'Hear, hear!' Imogen applauded halfheartedly, and

continued to wash up. She hoped she did know exactly where she was with Christian. It would be too completely shattering if she fell in love with him.

When she was in bed, she tried desperately to recall Raymond's image, his face, his voice, the personality which before Christian's coming that evening had seemed so real. But he eluded her. Nor could she conjure up any further ache for his loss. Instead she was haunted by a pair of mischievous blue eyes, and the memory of a thin, satirical mouth, which had pressed her own so masterfully.

Imogen's interview with her agent was depressing. Not only had he nothing on his books which might suit her, but he drew a dismal picture of the situation in her profession. Experienced dancers were queueing up by the dozen for the few parts obtainable.

'You'd better find something else to do while you're waiting,' he advised her, 'though I see little prospect of any improvement. I'll let you know if anything remotely possible turns up.'

So that was that.

'I'm afraid that's the end of our happy family,' Vivien said, when she told her of her abortive interview. 'At least you've something else to go to, and nothing lasts, it's said.'

'Let's hope Louise's marriage does,' Imogen remarked.

'Possibly it will, he's as commonplace as she is. It's we exotic blooms who get rapped. Perhaps we expect too much.'

'Raymond was all I wanted,' Imogen sighed.

'More fool you, he wasn't worth having. I hope you'll meet some glamorous Swede, who'll help you to forget him.' She looked at her friend slyly. 'In fact you've already met one.'

'Who is a worse proposition than Ray was,' Imogen

said bitterly. 'A girl can contend against female rivals, but not with slaloms and downhills.'

'Don't you worry about those, whatever they may be,' Vivien advised. 'Mother Nature hits back at even the most dedicated athlete.'

Christian came round that evening to discover how Imogen had progressed with her agent. Despondently she confessed that there was nothing doing, and she was prepared to go to Sweden if his sister still needed her services.

'She does,' he assured her, 'and as soon as possible.' Rather to her dismay he proposed departing in two days' time. Since she possessed a passport, there was nothing to wait for. Louise offered to see to the disposal of her few belongings, so there was no excuse for delay.

Christian then devoted his attention to Vivien, with whom he seemed smitten.

'Sure you wouldn't like me to come with you instead of Imo?' she asked him archly. 'Since she doesn't seem to be wildly enthusiastic.'

'I wouldn't dare to take you,' he declared. 'In a land of blondes you'd create a furore. Too great a responsibility, my dear.'

'But Imo isn't a blonde.'

'No, but she's an icicle,' he returned. 'You, I fancy, are quite the reverse.'

'Incandescent?' she suggested, laughing. 'Don't look so devastated, Imo. I don't care for other people's children and I'm going on tour.'

Imogen was not devastated, and knew Vivien was only joking, but she was struggling with a feeling of discomfort caused by Christian's and Vivien's easy familiarity. It could not be that she was jealous, and she knew it was all nonsense, but she did not like it, which was being petty and absurd. What did it matter to her if Christian found her friend alluring?

The next two days passed in a fever of preparation. Imogen paid a lightning visit to her parents, and discovered that Lettice had written to her mother giving a full account of her prospects, having been certain that Imogen would accept in the end. They seemed pleased that their daughter had a chance to repay the Wainwrights for all their kindness, an aspect of the situation which Imogen had rather overlooked, and her father trotted out the cliché about travel broadening the mind.

Lettice sent her a fur coat and a parka, which she said she had no further use for, and Imogen might find welcome in Jamtland. It was the beginning of March, and the snow had at last gone from the south at any rate, and Imogen's thoughts were turning springwards. The garments were a reminder that she would be returning to winter, and the sight of the heavy overcoat which Christian was carrying when he met her at the airport was unpleasantly suggestive.

However, when they touched down at Bromma at midday, the sun was shining brightly out of a cloudless blue sky, and the frost on the snow-covered buildings glittered like a myriad gems.

Christian had arranged for a taxi to meet them to drive into the city. They were not leaving until the evening, when they were to catch the night express for the north.

The car deposited them at a hotel opposite to the station, where Christian appeared to be well known, and the manager was agreeable to stowing their cases in the cloakroom, pending their departure.

After lunch, Christian announced that he had to go out to see an estate agent about Greta's flat, and left Imogen in the lounge to await his return for dinner.

The hotel like all those in Sweden, was spotlessly clean, centrally heated, double windowed and well furnished, but Imogen was too restless and excited to stay quietly put as Christian seemed to expect. Retrieving her fur coat, she went out into the sunlit streets.

Wandering down the broad Vasagaten, she came to water and a bridge which ran parallel to that carrying the railway. The air was very cold, but invigorating, and the sun gave some warmth. Giant ice-floes floated in the waterways, which were only just becoming free.

The bridge led her across into the historic centre of Stockholm. She turned left along the quayside, where another bridge led over to Helgeandsholmen and the Riksdagshusit, the Swedish Houses of Parliament. To her right was the Royal Palace, but this she did not identify. All she was aware of was massed buildings at different levels, with the spire of the German church pointing heavenwards, and a difficult assortment of street names.

Finally, feeling chilly and lost among the hurrying strangers, she retraced her steps to the Varsabron Bridge, which name she had managed to memorise, and the welcome warmth of the hotel, with a feeling of strong resentment against Christian for deserting her.

But when he did at length appear, she was so pleased to have someone to talk to that she forgot her former annoyance.

He was looking particularly handsome, the dark suit he was wearing showing up his fairness. Seeing him among his mother's people, she thought he looked more Scandinavian than English. She noticed the women in the lounge were all handsome, tall blondes, and she could understand why he found Vivien's dark beauty so attractive. She was also struck by their air of calm self-possession; these were level-headed women, who knew exactly what they wanted and meant to get it. It occurred to her that Christian must have found herself and her friends frivolous, not to say kittenish.

Noticing the direction of her eyes, Christian said:

'Throughout the historic period Sweden has remained almost exclusively in the possession of the original Germanic immigrants. Swedes are the most uniform type in Europe. You, my dear, with your ancestry of Briton, Celt, Saxon and Norman, are a mongrel.'

'I like that,' she exclaimed indignantly. 'What are you then? You have a British father.'

'Thanks for the reminder. I'm apt to forget I'm not all Swedish when I come back here.'

So it was not her imagination that he had become more Nordic since their arrival. Her heart sank a little. Would Greta be even more foreign? The aloofness of their companions in the hotel did not suggest the Swedes were a forthcoming race.

A young man came in, and recognising Christian, came up to them, bowing and holding out his hand.

'Herr Vainwright, is it not?'

Christian rose and returned the salutation. Then he introduced Imogen, and Herr Erik Bergquist repeated his performance.

'The lady is perhaps Herr Vainwright's affianced?' he said to Christian.

'It's not official yet,' Christian told him with a mischievous glint in his eyes.

They talked for a while about sport. Herr Bergquist, it seemed, was a reporter and wanted to congratulate Christian upon his recent successes and perhaps get a paragraph for his paper.

Christian excused himself, saying they must dine as they had to catch a train north.

When they were seated at a table in the dining-room, Imogen demanded to know why he had sought to mislead the young man.

'Why couldn't you say I was your sister's help?'

'Why should I? It isn't his business. Moreover, I didn't like the look in that young man's eye. Knowing your weakness, my dear, I didn't want to encourage him. Now he thinks you're booked.'

'Don't be ridiculous,' she told him sharply, irritated by his mocking air, 'and I'm not your dear!'

'No?' he grinned. 'I thought you aimed to be every man's dear.' She flushed with anger. 'Now don't spit at me. No doubt I misunderstood you. You're so inconsistent, my ... Imogen. But to return to Herr Redaktor Bergquist, I don't want him trailing after you to Jamtland.'

'As if he'd do that!'

'His job takes him everywhere, and you're a bit conspicuous among our blonde beauties.'

Wanting to distract him from discussing herself, she asked:

'I thought his name was Erik, not what you just called him.'

'Redaktor? Oh, that's his title. It means reporter. Everyone uses their title here. You will be Frocken Mother's Help Sinclair.'

'Doesn't sound very distinguished.' She laughed ruefully. 'But why?'

'Because they're a bit short of surnames in this country. In a city of a million people there could be ten thousand Karlssons, so you'll find them listed in the telephone directory under their professions, and every job is a profession, however humble, for it's a fiercely egalitarian society. Friend Erik would appear as Bergquist, Redaktor, Erik.'

'I see,' she said, hoping Greta would live up to the egalitarian concept.

They were served a substantial meal of soup, followed by smögasbord, a sort of hors d'oeuvres, which included various forms of fish, pickled herring, anchovy, shrimps, cold meats, vegetable salad and cheese. This was followed by the main course, chicken with mushrooms. Mushrooms, Christian told her, were a favourite food in that country, and were grown all the year round. They finished with an iced pudding, and coffee.

Feeling comfortably replete, Imogen would have welcomed sleep in a hotel bedroom, instead of having to wrap up and go out into the cold, and very black night. The bright lights of the station swam before her eyes, as they sought their sleeper. She was tired out with all her new impressions.

'Dropping on your feet, my ... I mean, poor girl,' Christian said kindly. 'Never mind, you can have a long sleep on the train, we don't arrive until morning.'

Quickly and efficiently they were shown into their reserved compartments. Christian uttered a cheerful, 'Goodnight, sleep well,' and removing her outer garments she tumbled into her berth. She was asleep almost as soon as her head touched the pillow.

CHAPTER SIX

CENTRAL SWEDEN is a land of lake and forest, sloping down to the Baltic from the Norwegian mountains, intersected by numerous rivers, which carry the timber which is its chief industry down to the sea.

As it was night, Imogen saw nothing of the country through which the train was travelling. She slept heavily for the first few hours, and then became wakeful, aware that she was both nervous and apprehensive. What, she wondered, had led her to embark upon this mad adventure? Alone, in the rushing dark, she faced the truth. It was neither the need for work—she could have found that anywhere—nor a wish to oblige the Wainwrights, which had brought her here, but a desire to see Christian's other country and to meet his sister, simply because it was his other country and she was his sister. She had been motivated by a subconscious urge to strengthen the links between herself and him. What she felt for him was not antagonism but attraction, and she had been incredibly foolish to yield to it.

By her own act, she had destroyed any liking he might have had for her, deliberately presenting herself to him as a heartless coquette from their first moment of meeting. His behaviour over Peter showed only too clearly that he had accepted her as such, and he had never ceased to taunt her about it, as the incident with Herr Bergquist had illustrated. But even if she could make him reverse his opinion of her, and he had once said she could be a nice girl, the situation was quite hopeless. For she had a greater rival than any woman in the sport to which he was dedicated. Neither Erica's kittenish charm nor Vivien's beauty could tempt him from his allegiance to it. He had told her frankly that he would never contemplate marriage until he was done with racing. Against the lure of the ski-run a mere girl did not count.

Now she had landed herself among strangers in a foreign land, and in a few days' time he would be gone.

And a good thing too, she consoled herself, if I see much more of him, I shall commit the unpardonable folly of becoming too fond of him. The rhythm of the train echoed the warning words of the song: 'Men were deceivers ever.'

It was still dark when they reached their destination, though the eastern horizon was streaked with light. A setting moon threw a ghostly light over black pines and shimmering ice on a wide lake. Everything was covered in snow and it was bitterly cold.

A car with chained wheels had come to meet them, and Imogen huddled into the fur-lined wraps with which it was supplied as it clanked over the snow-packed road.

The stocky peasant who was driving it talked to Christian in his native tongue, and the incomprehensible words added to the unreality of the scene. It could not be herself, Imogen Sinclair, who had left civilisation to come to this semi-Arctic outpost with the idea of living here. She could not have been so mad.

They passed no villages, nor even houses, the country seemed quite empty. Once she burst out:

'Does no one live here?'

'It's sparsely populated,' Christian told her, 'and will become more so. There is an unending drift to the south.'

'I'm not surprised,' Imogen said, shivering.

They came to a lumber camp, where a roaring fire of brushwood lit the scene with lurid light. Piles of tree trunks lined the roadside, waiting to be transported. A group of wooden buildings stood in a clearing, and a vast sledge piled with logs was slowly moving away drawn by a sno-mobile. The lumbermen in fur jackets and parkas looked like denizens of the underworld in the ruddy glow from the fire, and the scream of a circular saw was a diabolical accompaniment.

'They tip the logs down a chute on to the river,' Christian told her. 'There they are piled up so that when the ice thaws the water carries them down to factories on the coast.'

'Do you mean they have to work out here all winter?' Imogen asked incredulously.

'Winter is the time to fell,' he explained, 'when no sap is rising, and the snow facilitates transport. When the summer comes, most of these boys will go back to work on the farms where they come from.'

'They must be tough!' she exclaimed.

'True descendants of the Vikings,' he suggested. 'We're a tough nation.'

The trees thinned out into snow-covered fields, and the farmhouse came into view—deep-eaved, to protect it from snow, small-windowed to exclude draughts and long and low to escape the winter gales, but the windows were blazing with light and Imogen sighed thankfully, realising that at least there was plenty of electricity.

If Christian had seemed more Nordic when he reached Sweden, Greta was determined to appear English. She greeted Imogen warmly, while her two flaxen-haired tots of three and four murmured shyly, '*Valkomna.*' Christian lifted each in turn, exclaiming at their increase in growth, while Greta laughed, and said he was imagining it, since it was only a short while since he had seen them and babies did not grow that fast.

'But you must be starved,' she said. 'Come and eat.'

She was a tall girl, flaxen-haired and very like her brother.

She led the way into the living-room, a big room, all in wood, stained and painted. The low ceiling was supported by thick beams, the walls were polished pine wood, the floor bare boards except for several strips of peasant matting woven from coloured rags. At one end was an enormous open fireplace, upon which huge logs blazed, at the other was a covered round white stove. A wooden refectory table was set for a meal, with carved chairs set around it.

It was so warm, that Imogen loosened her coat.

'Perhaps you would like to take that off,' Greta suggested. 'I'll show you your room.'

Reluctantly Imogen followed her anticipating an ice-cold bedroom, but the little room into which she was shown was also heated by a closed stove. This again was all in wood, with the simplest of pinewood furniture.

'The bath and loo are next door,' Greta said frankly. 'The plumbing is not up to Ritz standard, but we manage. There is a sauna bath-house, but we only use that in the summer.'

She went, and Imogen was aware of the utter silence surrounding the farm. She was relieved when it was broken by a cock crowing.

When she returned to the living-room, Greta and Christian were talking about the sports at Åre.

'So long as you don't expect us to come and watch,' Greta was saying. 'It's much too cold.' She saw Imogen hesitating in the doorway. 'Come along and sit down. Make yourself at home.'

Greta served out bowls of porridge, which her children called *gröt*. Imogen normally loathed porridge, but she was so hungry she ate it with appetite. This was followed by fried ham and rye bread, very crisp and hard, Swedish *knäckebrod* made in flat cakes.

'You'll miss all this space,' Christian said, looking round the big room. 'I saw your Stockholm flat yesterday, four small rooms and a kitchen, not room to swing a cat.'

'Who wants to swing a cat?' Greta returned. 'It'll be just heaven after this barn, and we'll get our summer a month earlier.' She turned to Imogen. 'It doesn't pretend to get warm here until the middle of June.'

Imogen shivered. It was then only March.

'Exactly,' Christian observed. 'I've only come for the snow.'

'I know that, and if you've finished, you'd better go and hone and wax your skis. That'll keep you from under my feet.'

Christian looked with mock hurt at Imogen.

'You see what a welcome my sister gives me after travelling all these miles to visit her!'

'I thought you said you'd only come for the snow,' she reminded him.

'*Et tu, Brute!*' He took himself off laughing.

Imogen helped Greta to clear the table.

'He's just like all the others,' she said of her brother. 'Never marry a Swede, Imogen—I may call you that? They're all egoists, cold and unappreciative, absorbed in their own work and ambitions.'

'But your brother isn't Swedish.'

'Oh, he's technically British since he was born on the other side of the North Sea, but he shares many of my dear departed's failings. I can't pretend to mourn very deeply for Sven. He expected me to be just a housekeeper and a bedmate. It wasn't good enough.'

'But isn't that all most wives are?' Imogen asked, feeling a little embarrassed by these revelations.

'But I'm educated, Imogen, I can speak five languages, drive a Volvo in a motor rally, entertain as a hostess. I need more scope than baking cakes and washing the kitchen floor. Once I get down south I can use my talents.'

'And the children?'

'They'll go to a nursery school.'

Imogen was slightly shocked by this declaration of female independence, but she said nothing.

Greta looked at her slyly. 'Don't look so disapproving,' she remonstrated. 'Christian told me you came from swinging London, so you should understand.'

'When did he tell you that?' Imogen asked, surprised.

'When he first described you. He writes occasionally, you know.' She dimpled. 'He wrote quite a lot about you.'

Imogen hoped she was not blushing. 'Really?' she murmured faintly.

'You've made an impression, but take my advice. Have an affair if you want to, you know we don't believe in repressions here, but don't, whatever you do, marry him.'

This idea was so improbable that Imogen was able to laugh without embarrassment. 'Such a thought would never occur to either of us,' she said with conviction.

Greta looked disbelieving. 'Although he's brought you all this way to meet me?' she insinuated.

In a sudden flash, Imogen remembered what Christian had said about Erica. To bring her to Jamtland would put ideas into her head, but regarding herself, he had declared she would be under no such misapprehension.

'I thought he brought me to help you,' she observed, 'though you don't seem to need me.'

'But I do, you don't know how much. Just having someone to talk to ... why, I feel better already. And there'll be a lot to do, so much to sort out. Don't take any notice of what I said about my brother. I've probably got it all wrong.'

Imogen assured her that she had.

The sun came out about midday and the whole land-scape was bathed in brilliant light, in which each bough and twig of the birch trees planted round the house stood out in microscopic clarity. There was none of the mistiness which shrouds an English scene, all the outlines were hard under the azure sky and upon every flat surface, the snow gleamed. In spite of its beauty, Imogen regarded the view disconsolately. She had seen such a lot of snow that winter and she was longing for the sight of green grass.

Christian on the other hand was revelling in it. The weather promised well for the sports meeting. He was out testing the snow on skis for most of the day, and checking his equipment.

'I've been away too long,' he complained. 'Domestic cares have played havoc with my form.'

'There'll be nothing up to your standard at Åre,' Greta comforted him. 'You know you only go there for sentimental reasons.' He was entered as a soloist.

'Well, it'll get me into trim for Spain, and my trainer will be there. Tomorrow I must put in some serious practice, and the day after I'll be leaving you, Sis. I'll be staying there to take advantage of every moment of good weather.'

Imogen's heart sank. The inevitable parting was so near.

She had little time for repining, as she was busy about the house, learning the way things were done and try-ing to make friends with little Kajsa and Sven, so called for his father. They seemed to her to be too quiet and repressed, and very different from Lettice's boisterous couple. No wonder Christian had been con-cerned about them. He too had noticed the contrast. Their mother's viewpoint was different.

'It's never too soon for children to learn to be quiet and have good manners,' she proclaimed. 'The things we dislike most here are dirt, disorder and noise.'

Small though they were, the two children went out into the brief sunshine, each with his and her little sledge, bundled up in coats, shawls, mittens and boots, so that Kajsa looked like a roly-poly.

The child fell on any icy patch, and screamed loudly. Regardless of the cold, Imogen ran out just as she was to pick her up and carry her indoors.

'Any damage?' Greta asked.

'I don't think so.' Imogen was unwinding the voluminous outer coverings. 'A bruise, perhaps, and she's scared.'

'Then stop blubbering, Kajsa,' commanded the Spartan mother. 'You've nothing to cry about.'

But Imogen saw the hurt of rejection in the drowned blue eyes, and gathered the small body close into her arms.

'There, darling, it was a nasty tumble, but you're all right now.'

Greta laughed and went into her office where she did the estate accounts, but Imogen remained with the child on her lap, continuing to soothe her. Kajsa put her arms round her neck and clung to her passionately, and the girl's face grew soft and tender with solicitude, until, looking up, she became aware that Christian had come in and was watching her with an enigmatical expression.

Hastily she put the child down, and drew her wraps about her.

'All right now, darling? Then go back to your play.'

'You needn't try to hide your light under a bushel,' he observed, watching his niece's retreating figure.

'Now what exactly do you mean by that?' she challenged him.

'No need to ruffle up, because I caught you off your

118

guard!'

'I'm not normally soppy,' she said hurriedly, for an unexpected tenderness in his look was discomposing her. 'But those kids seem starved for love.'

'I told you they were,' he reminded her. 'Greta's hard, but she has some reason to be. Sven gave her a poor deal. Having installed her in this back of beyond, he absented himself in the winter, leaving her to hold the fort. What he was up to was anybody's guess—he said he was working with the timber gangs—but I have my doubts and so had Greta. It's not altogether a picnic alone here in midwinter when it's only daylight for an hour or two and the temperature well below zero.'

'So she isn't exactly grieving for his loss?'

'Would you?' he returned, and went back outside.

So Greta's late husband was yet another example of male depravity, Imogen thought grimly.

Christian was away all the next day, but returned for the evening meal and seemed in high spirits. Imogen watched him wistfully. It would be a long while before they spent another evening together. She noticed he seemed to be studying her with a curiously intent expression and wondered if he was thinking she was not making out. But if at this late date he was having doubts about her efficiency, it was his mistake, not hers. She had never pretended to be domesticated.

When she returned to the living-room after putting the children to bed, he put down the paper he was reading and asked if she would like to come out for a drive.

Astonished, Imogen stared at him. 'At this time of night? It's dark and cold.'

'There's a moon and I thought you might like to sample a sledge ride. Very romantic things, sledges.'

He was looking at her with a slightly mocking expression, and she regarded him doubtfully, suspecting that he was making fun of her unfamiliarity with the country's customs.

'Are they a speciality about here?' she asked uncertainly.

'No more so than in many other snowbound lands, but they are rapidly becoming obsolete. Sno-mobiles and sno-cars are taking their place, so you'd better avail yourself of the chance of sampling one before Greta's horses are sent to the knackers.'

'As if I'd ever permit that!' Greta protested, 'but since Christian's being so accommodating'—she gave Imogen a meaning look—'why not take advantage of his offer?'

'I always feel the need of a little recreation before a race,' Christian announced cryptically, and as Imogen still hesitated, added: 'Who knows? I might come to grief on the Areskutan run, and I'm sure you'd be devastated to think that you'd refused my last request.'

Imogen's eyes darkened with sudden fear. Skiing could, she realised, be dangerous to life and limb, something which she had not fully appreciated before.

'Is it so dangerous?' she asked anxiously.

'No more so than most sports.' He swung himself to his feet. 'Go and put on your warmest things while I harness the horses.'

Greta was smiling mischievously. 'Be careful,' she warned. 'Moonlight too can be dangerous.' She was not thinking of skiing.

Visions of dalliance on warm summer nights floated before Imogen's eyes, but outside it was freezing.

'Not in this cold,' she said lightly, and went to put on her outdoor clothes, with a pleasurable surge of excitement.

Fur-lined boots, fur coat, mittens and parka made her look as much of a bundle as Kajsa had done, and hardly seductive with only her eyes visible above the woollen scarf which she wound round her face, but she did not suspect Christian of any amorous intentions. It was just one of his sudden whims, and he could never bear to be indoors if there was anything he could do outside. But she would be alone with him, perhaps for the last time, and that was sufficient inducement to face even frostbite.

But there seemed to be no risk of that, for the low-slung sledge was filled with fur-lined rugs, into which she could snuggle. It was drawn by two Norwegian horses, shaggy beasts of an unusual pinkish colour, which looked white in the moonlight. Two ancient carriage lamps were fixed on either side.

'Which must have come out of the Ark,' Christian commented, 'but we shan't meet anything at this time of night.'

The sledge skimmed easily down the track hardened by the passage of the farm vehicles with hardly a sound, the horses' sharpened hooves made no noise, being muffled by the snow. The road lay through a wood, with trees rising straight and tall on either side of it, black sentinels against the luminous sky. There was no wind to disturb the stillness, and the air was keen with frost.

'Better than Sven's old car,' Christian said with satisfaction.

'What have you done with yours?' Imogen asked idly. She was very conscious of him sitting beside her, big and bulky in his fur-lined coat, his keen profile sharply etched against the piled snow, thrown up by the plough into high banks on either side of them.

'Put it into store. I'll probably bring it out next summer. Joe can borrow it for his holidays. I find the trains are better for long distances at this time of the year.'

The road ascended a sharp rise, the trees cleared, and they went down towards the arm of a lake. It stretched like a silver sheet before them, with the humped shape of a fir-crowned island black against the night sky.

'For motor traffic the lakes are better going than the land,' Christian observed.

'You mean you can drive over them?'

'Why not? The ice is sound enough. You'll see buses using them to shorten what in summer is a circuitous route. Incidentally, our power stations here are built underground so that they can use the flow of water which runs beneath the ice, when the surface is frozen.'

'What efficient people the Swedes are!'

'They pride themselves on making everything work.'

Instructive comments about the country, and she had been hoping for some more personal conversation! Yet what could she expect him to talk about? The morrow's ordeal? He had come out to forget about that.

He pulled up the horses.

'Let's walk down to the lake.'

Somewhat reluctantly she crept out of her warm nest of fur, while Christian tied the horses to a tree stump, and flung a rug over each of them. Taking her arm, he led her down to the edge of the lake. The almost eerie stillness wrapped them round in a magic world of glittering white in which no creature stirred; they might have been the last living couple left on earth.

Then suddenly, points of quivering fire appeared along the northern horizon, and shot up into the sky like golden rockets. The whole arc of the heavens shook with luminous green light. The strange fire trembled, sank into a bed of crimson and mauve, then rose again.

'What is it?' Imogen gasped, clutching Christian's arm, for the illumination was uncanny.

'Haven't you heard of the Aurora Borealis?'

'Of course, the Northern Lights!' she exclaimed, relieved. 'I'm glad to have seen it,' she shivered, 'if only it wasn't so cold.'

He turned to her and deliberately unwound the scarf from her face. Then she was enclosed in a bear-like hug and his mouth came down hers. A wild ecstasy thrilled her, and she clung to him, giving back kiss for kiss, until, spent, she lay back in his arms, and became aware that he was laughing.

'I can't get at you through all those clothes,' he complained. 'but I hope you're warmer now.'

A lump rose in her throat. He was only playing with her! This was the relaxation he sought before going into action. Weakly she tried to extricate herself. but his hold tightened.

'Imogen,' he said softly against her ear, 'little green-eyed witch, for you have bewitched me, you know.' He kissed her again. 'Could you bear to live here always?'

'That depends who I had to live with,' she murmured.

'With me, of course.' He hesitated, then blurted out: 'Will you marry me?'

He could not really have said it. His words were a product of her own wishful thinking. Dazedly, she questioned:

'What did you say?'

'You heard. I know we haven't known each other very long, but does that matter, when we feel as we do?'

So he *had* said it. Sheer astonishment kept her dumb, while he went on rapidly, as if he wanted to get the words out before he repented of them: 'I warn you I shan't make a good husband. I can't promise to settle down ... yet, but eventually, we might have a place like this. Materially I'm not badly off, you'll lack for nothing.'

'I can't believe you really want to marry me,' she said ingenuously, too surprised to prevaricate. 'Why?'

'Why does a man want to marry a woman?' he returned almost roughly, 'because it's the only way to get you ... isn't it?'

With a little sigh, she drew herself away from him, and he did not restrain her. That last question was more what she expected from him.

'I wouldn't settle for anything less,' she told him proudly, and wondered if she spoke the truth. She knew now that she was hopelessly in love with him. As that fantastic light had blazed up in the sky, so had her own feelings suddenly flared into recognition. He was everything to her, the beginning and the end. Life without him would be a desert. The emotion which Raymond had aroused in her was a mere candleflame to a bonfire compared to that which now engulfed her, but, even to keep him, could she bring herself to become a mere mistress?

She knew there had been wisdom in Greta's advice that they should confine their relationship to an affair. Christian was not wholly hers. He had other urges which might prove too strong for her to combat, but all her instincts were prompting her to take all he offered, to bind him to her whatever the consequences. The tremendous surge of emotion which was flooding her whole being was too precious to cheapen by a transitory liaison, and that he could suggest it was hurtful.

'I suppose you said that because you think I'm easy?' she said reproachfully.

'That was your own assessment of yourself, and one which I never accepted,' he replied. 'It was for your own sake that I wondered if we should risk a permanent union. You may not find me very easy to live with, but if you're game, I'd much prefer it that way.'

'I'm willing to take a gamble on you, Christian,' she said with a little laugh of pure happiness. 'That is, if you're sure you mean it,' she added anxiously. 'It isn't just the moonlight?'

'Yes, I do mean it,' he assured her almost fiercely, 'though...' he laughed, 'the moonlight helps. I want you, Imogen, most damnably. You thought I was a brute when I made you toil up Rushup Edge, didn't you? But it was then that I discovered you were more than just another pretty girl. You had determination, spirit—you were the sort of woman I would like to mother my sons.'

So he must be in earnest if he was thinking about children, but there was a catch in it. Instinctively she drew further away from him.

'Does my frankness offend you?' he asked. 'Wouldn't you like to have our son?'

'To be trained to be a champion skier?' she asked with an edge to her voice.

'Not necessarily, though of course I would like him to be a good sportsman.' He reached for her again, gathering her close in his arms. 'You hate the skiing, don't you? But it's my only vice.'

'I only hate it because it takes you away from me.'

'But it can't do that, Imogen, and a time will come when I shall be past it.'

'And then you'll fall back upon your wife?'

'Of course.' He laughed, refusing to take her antagonism seriously. 'I'll need a compensation.'

'Is that all...' she was beginning indignantly, but he stopped her mouth. Under his kiss she could neither think nor remonstrate. After all, she would have her compensations too.

Presently he raised his head, and asked:

'Perhaps now you will tell me why you had to put on that act, pretending to be the man-eater you aren't and never could be.'

Somewhat haltingly she told him about Raymond and the distrust of men he had engendered in her, feeling that she was relating something which had happened in another life.

When she had finished, he asked jealously:

'Did you really love him?'

'I thought I did,' she said honestly, 'but I know now it was only an adolescent romance. It wasn't in the least like what I feel for you.'

'I should hope not!'

His mouth closed on hers again possessively. In the northern sky the lights throbbed, rose and sank. The setting moon drew a silver path across the ice while huge stars brightened in the darkening heavens—a strange, wild setting for her newly awakened love, and somehow fitting for her Viking lover.

Many questions still lurked below her consciousness, the how, the why, the wherefore, but at that moment she was content to accept the miracle which had happened without criticism. At the very moment in which the overwhelming nature of her love had been revealed to her, she had discovered that it was returned. And yet there was still a little niggling doubt; anxiously she asked:

'I was let down once, but you'll never let me down?'

'I'm not a cad,' he said briefly.

With his arm about her, he led her away from the lake, back to the waiting horses, who were snorting and stamping. He helped her into the sledge, wrapping the rugs about her with almost tender care.

As they drove back through the black and silver night, Imogen began to feel an increasing reluctance to face his sister with their news.

Greta had already warned her against marrying Christian; she was sure to be critical and disapproving. That her own marriage had been unhappy had no doubt made her biased against matrimony. Imogen felt that she could not bear to have her new found ecstasy and joy marred by a third party's misgivings, and Christian would not be there to support her.

Hesitantly she asked:

'Must we tell Greta now? I . . . I'd rather leave it for a while. After all, I've only just arrived, and I came to help her, not to get engaged to you.'

'You came because I wanted you to come,' he told her. 'Why else do you think I went to the trouble and expense of bringing you to Jamtland? Greta could have found someone nearer at hand.'

This revelation astonished her. 'Then you cared before . . .' she gasped.

'I suppose I did. All I knew was I couldn't bear to lose sight of you. Installed with Greta I knew I'd got you just where I wanted you.'

'You scheming wretch!' she exclaimed, laughing. Even then it did not occur to her that there had been one omission in the night's confessions. Christian had not declared his own love. Nor had the word been mentioned between them in regard to their own feelings.

'You can hardly expect your sister to appreciate your point of view,' she said lightly.

'Perhaps not,' he agreed. 'But maybe you're right and it would be easier for you, at any rate, if we keep mum for the present. Greta might try to put you against me.'

'She could never do that,' Imogen assured him.

'Unfortunately I shall have to leave you for a while, so I shall be unable to defend myself,' he told her. 'But you knew that. When I get back from the Pyrenees, you'll be in Stockholm. I'll come to you there, and we'll see about getting married.'

'So soon?'

'Is there anything to wait for?'

'I suppose not.' She had not anticipated such a lightning romance; weddings needed preparation—or did they?

'Where would we live?' she asked breathlessly.

'Oh, we'll have a hut in the woods throughout the

summer. That's a good old Swedish custom. The forests are very beautiful. Afterwards we'll be travelling, I expect, but instead of going off to the Andes, I want to devote the summer to you.'

Their future sounded a little unsettled, she thought, with all a woman's desire for a permanent home, but the prospect of having Christian to herself throughout the summer alone in the forest was very alluring. But after the summer, came the winter, and the snow...

'That's very noble of you,' she said with a touch of sarcasm. 'Do I take it you'll be a summer husband only?'

'By no means, but you won't expect me to give up the skiing?' he asked anxiously.

'No, Christian, I know what it means to you.' But even as she spoke she felt a qualm of misgiving. Must she always take second place to his sport?

'You'll come with me on my tours, of course. You haven't seen a ski-race yet.'

'I'd love to see one.' But her tone lacked conviction. At that moment she hated his preoccupation with racing.

So when they reached the farm, she enthused about the spectacle which they had seen, but mentioned nothing more personal. Looking at her flushed cheeks and shining eyes, Greta smiled knowingly, and uneasily Imogen wondered what she was thinking, though she was sure she did not suspect the truth.

Christian left next morning early, and was so curt and tense during breakfast that Imogen felt that she must have dreamed the episode of the previous night. Seeing, but not understanding, her blank bewilderment, Greta whispered to her that he was always like this before a race, an unwelcome reminder that the women in Christian's life took second place to his skis. He kissed her when he left, but it was no more than the fraternal salute which he gave to his sister, and as such, Greta did not notice it.

The time that followed was a blank. Imogen had been strung to the highest pitch of emotion by the lake, but now reaction set in and she was assailed by doubt, misgiving and resentment. Christian should not have left her in a void without reassurance. That her trouble was partly her own fault was no consolation. If she told Greta about it, the engagement would have had more reality, but she did not feel strong enough to face the arguments against it which she felt sure she would bring forth.

Meanwhile she had plenty to do, helping Greta to pack her possessions and looking after the children.

The farm possessed a television set, which worked efficiently except during blizzards. There were no storms during the Åre Sports Week and they were able to watch the events, most of which Imogen found rather dull; she had never had much interest in watching sport. There was skating, curling, sledging, even running. But Christian's appearances were disappointing. Disguised by a black racing helmet, and goggles, he was only identifiable by the number on his chest and back, being only one of a number of similar tall figures in spider pants.

Imogen saw him in the slalom, a dark shadow descending, against the snow, gliding between the gates, making the intricate turns with perfect precision, as he had once described it to her. She raised a little excitement while they were waiting for the times to be announced, but even when Christian was hailed winner, he only took off his goggles and raised his plexiglass face mask. It might have been he or half a dozen others.

Mid-week he rang up. Greta took the call, as the telephone was in her office. She shouted to Imogen, 'He wants to speak to you!' But she did not leave the room, and stood hovering.

Imogen heard Christian's voice with a note in it which she had never heard before.

'Missing me?'

'But of course.' Constrained by Greta's presence, she had to guard her speech. 'How's it going? We saw the slalom. Congratulations.' Not at all what she wanted to say.

'The mountain race is the big event,' he told her. 'I'm working hard and the snow's perfect. I did the Areskutan run in four minutes—if only I can maintain that speed when I'm competing, I'll beat the record.'

Involuntarily she sighed. There was so much else she wanted him to say, but his thoughts were running on beating records.

'Are you alone?' he asked.

'Greta's here.'

Greta grabbed the receiver. 'Yes, Christian?' she queried.

Imogen moved away. Greta had thought that he wanted to speak to her again and the message, if he had had one for her ear alone, was unuttered.

The big race was a disappointment. It was not easy to televise. They saw the masked figures on their way up, they saw the finish. One by one the black figures skimmed into the finishing oval, were acclaimed by the crowd, their times announced. Finally it was given out in four languages: Christian Wainwright, time, four minutes. He had won! Then at long last she did see him plainly, for in his exuberance he tore off helmet and mask, as his excited supporters raised him on their shoulders. Yearningly she gazed at the image of that proud Viking head, the beloved face, so utterly indifferent, absorbed in a triumph in which she had no part.

That was in the afternoon. All evening Imogen waited in a fever of anticipation. He had promised to give them a look before going on to Spain. But bedtime arrived without his appearance.

'Too busy celebrating,' Greta decided. 'Several members of the team were there. He must have taken the night train south with them. We shan't see him again until we're installed in Stockholm.'

She was neither hurt nor surprised, her brother's movements were always unpredictable, but Imogen felt sick with disappointment. Christian's behaviour was casual in the extreme. Was it possible he was regretting his impulsive proposal by the lake?

Monday morning brought a letter. Imogen opened the typewritten envelope without much curiosity, and the unfamiliar handwriting puzzled her for a moment until she glanced at the signature. It gave her a little shock to realise that she had never seen Christian's calligraphy before, bringing home to her how little she really knew about him. She returned it to its envelope to read when she was alone, glancing surreptitiously at Greta, who, to her relief, was too occupied with her own mail to be interested in Imogen's.

'Good!' Greta exclaimed, looking up from the sheet she was perusing. 'The decorations to the flat are finished and we can move in. You can't know how thankful I'll be to see the back of this place!'

Imogen glanced round the polished pinewood walls. 'Yet it's rather lovely,' she said.

'You haven't been here in November,' Greta told her, 'when the first snow comes and it's never really light with the prospect of months of frost in front of one. I bet most of the snow is melted in Stockholm already.'

There was still plenty outside on the farm, and the children, at Imogen's suggestion, went to sort out their sledges and skates. What was to be taken and what left behind. It seemed ages to her before she could find an excuse to escape into her bedroom to read her letter.

It was not very long. Christian apologised for the hasty scrawl, and for not being able to call at the farm on his way south. There had been a sudden change of plans and he had had to leave at once. He would see her ere long in Stockholm, and with the skiing season nearly over they would be able to plan their future.

'There's lots more I want to say, but I've no time,' he concluded, and merely signed himself: 'Yours, Christian.'

The last two words were so scribbled that they suggested an interruption, but even so, it was a poor effort for a first love letter, in fact it was not a love letter at all. Remembering the passionate notes Raymond had been able to pour out when it suited him, she returned it to its envelope with a sense of deprivation. True, she and Ray had been a pair of emotional teenagers, and Christian was adult and no scribe, but even so, his letter seemed chill and formal.

A sudden memory devastated her. Peter Lethwaite had said: 'He lets himself get carried away by moonlight and a pretty face and then spends the next day wondering how he can explain that he didn't mean what he said.'

There had been moonlight, with the Aurora Borealis for good measure, and he had been carried away. Slowly the chilling doubt spread over her thoughts. Daylight and a return to his beloved sport had changed Christian's mind. He was wondering how to extricate himself from an engagement he no longer desired.

CHAPTER SEVEN

ONCE she was installed in the Stockholm flat, Imogen's brief stay in the north became like a phantasma, a glimpse of an unfamiliar world seen on television or at the theatre, while the night by the lake had all the unreality of a fantasy. In dreams she often saw again that flaming sky, the frozen water glittering under the light of the moon, the dark shapes of the trees, but it had become remote and insubstantial. She felt that she had not actually been there.

Life in the flat was a setting with which she was familiar, the confined space—there were four rooms besides the kitchen and usual offices, Greta said when they had a visitor, Imogen would have to sleep with the children—streets and shops, which though different from London, were her normal background.

The week following Christian's departure had been one of confusion and bustle—establishing the manager, who was to take charge of the farm until it was sold, disposing of unwanted articles, packing the remainder—the long journey south, calming and comforting overtired children, whose world was being rent asunder. That period became a mass of blurred impressions in Imogen's mind, through which ran a thread of pain, for Christian did not write again and she desperately wanted his reassurance to dispel her doubts, to tell her that he had meant all he had said by the lake.

Sometimes she could almost convince herself that she had imagined the whole incident out of her wishful thinking, and even that was less painful than the growing certainty that Christian was regretting his impulsive proposal. Greta's complete unconsciousness of the situation made it appear all the more improbable, and as each day passed, it became more impossible to enlighten her. In fact Imogen was glad that she did not know; to see her first incredulity change to pity would have lacerated her pride.

For the Spanish sports meeting was over and Christian did not return to Stockholm. He sent them all gaily coloured postcards from the mountain resort where he had been competing. She had seen occasional flashes, televised of slaloms and downhills and ski-jumps, events which Imogen was beginning to dislike intensely. They were enemies to her love. Christian was occupied with the number of points he was winning to the exclusion of all thoughts of her. She doubted he would remember that she existed, but when he did not come, she surmised he had remembered her existence all too vividly, and wished to avoid her.

In Stockholm, the snow had melted, the waterways were free, though Greta warned that there could be further snowfalls.

'If I remember rightly from my childhood, you often have snow at Easter in England,' she pointed out, at Imogen's dismayed expression.

The flat had been redecorated prior to their occupation and all the furniture was new. Greta had brought nothing with her from her former life. Most of it was in whitewood. The apartment was immaculate and speckless with all the latest labour-saving devices. Imogen's principal chore was looking after the children. She took them out in the afternoons, and being used to the empty lands of mid-Sweden, they were awestruck by the bright, busy streets, the throngs of people and the procession of traffic.

They never tired of window-shopping and nothing delighted them more than to be taken round one of the glittering departmental stores.

Kajsa said: 'There can't be enough people in the world to buy all these lovely, lovely things.'

'There seems to be lots and lots of people here,' Sven remarked, looking at the passers-by.

Both children were bi-lingual, speaking English as well as they did their native tongue.

'We have to be,' Greta had explained. 'No one outside Sweden speaks Swedish, so English or German is our second language. These children will have a good start at school as I've ensured that they can talk my language.'

Imogen bought them small gifts from time to time, or gave them tea at a café, which delighted them.

Coming home from one of these expeditions, Greta met them with the information that her brother had been on the phone, and Imogen's heart leaped. Was Christian coming at last?

'It seems he's been involved in a spot of bother,' Greta informed her. 'A car he and several friends were travelling in met with an accident. The driver, a special pal of his, has been committed for trial. Very arbitary, these Spanish policemen—Christian as a principal witness is waiting for the case to come on and is very indignant about the way in which his friend has been treated. He says, however'—Greta smiled mischievously—'there's still good skiing in the Pyrenees.'

'He wasn't hurt himself?' Imogen asked anxiously.

'Only a few bruises.' Greta was helping Kajsa out of her outdoor clothes. 'He sent you his love,' she added carelessly. That was something, Imogen thought, but Greta spoilt it almost at once, by saying: 'In England you always send your love, where here we would say kind regards. Kajsa, don't wriggle.' She handed the child's anorak to Imogen, who had been assisting Sven.

'I wonder if there's a skirt involved,' she went on

casually, 'some of those women competitors are hand-some girls. In that case, we shan't see Christian until he's become tired of her and wants to escape.'

An observation which Imogen found particularly depressing, suspecting as she did that Christian was keeping away from her because he wanted to escape the consequences of his folly. If the story about the accident were true, he could at least have written to her, but, she reflected bitterly, letters were compromising. All she received was another gaudy postcard with a scrawled message. Postcards being more or less public property, she could hardly expect him to be amorous upon the back of one—besides, Greta might see it. The scribbled message informed her that she might expect to see him any day soon, and he gave no address. She looked disconsolately at the scene it depicted, snow-capped mountains under a cobalt-blue sky, the barrier that lay between her and him. It was symbolical.

Greta dropped her own pictorial representation on the table, remarking: 'I suppose it's something to get these. Christian declares that the telephone is the quickest and most efficient method of communication, and he has no use for what he calls chit-chat letters.'

But Imogen had been out when he rang up.

'You said he wrote to you when he was in Derby-shire,' she reminded Greta.

'Yes, there were various business matters to settle, and he made an effort because he knew I was lonely,' Greta explained.

Imogen digested this information in silence. That she might be lonely and in need of consolation did not seem to have occurred to him. Nor did he appear to want to hear from her. Second-hand information via Greta on the telephone had satisfied him, and her con-clusions were ominous; his sister meant more to him than she did.

His absence seemed much longer to her, waiting

anxiously for some sign of his continued affection, than it actually was. He, being immersed in his own affairs, did not notice the time slipping by, and since she was where he wanted her to be, as he had told her, he imagined a message on a postcard would content her.

Uncertainty drove the colour from her cheeks and put dark marks beneath her eyes. Greta said worriedly that she was afraid Stockholm did not suit her.

Imogen returned that she would be all right when the weather became warmer, and spring was on the way.

Slowly the city was waking from its long sleep, for it was first and foremost a summer town. The harbour was full of shipping plying between the islands upon which it was built, and the children loved a steamer trip. Green appeared in the parks and the sun shone brightly. Occasionally there was a flurry of snowflakes, but they did not lie.

One afternoon, Imogen was for once alone in the flat, Greta having taken the children to see some Olsson relatives. She took the opportunity of a free period to catch up with her correspondence. At long last she wrote the promised letter to Peter Lethwaite, hoping that by now he would no longer be concerned about her relations with Christian, and she took care to mention that he was away. She sighed as she directed the envelope, wishing she could write to Christian. Castleton seemed very far away.

The chime of the doorbell interrupted her and a faint excitement stirred in her, as it always did when an unexpected caller rang. There was always the chance that it might be Christian.

She threw a hasty glance at the mirror on the wall and ran a comb through her hair, which she had rumpled in the throes of composition. She was thinner, her eyes looked larger, and her white costume emphasised her slenderness. She needed some make-up, but there was no time to attend to that. Anyway, she was being optimistic to imagine that the chime portended other than a message for Greta.

She went hastily to the door as a second chime echoed through the flat, and opening it, found herself confronting Raymond Benito.

Astonishment rendered her speechless, she could only gape at him, while he smiled at her triumphantly.

'Surprised?' he asked. 'I called at your old digs and found Lou in possession. Fancy old Lou being the first of you to wed—but then she wasn't as choosey as you and Viv.' He was talking to cover a slight embarrassment. 'She gave me your address and said you were working here.' Then as she neither moved nor spoke, he added anxiously: 'Have I arrived at an awkward moment? Can I come in?'

Mechanically she stood aside so that he could enter the flat, while she tried to register the fact that this good-looking stranger was her once familiar friend, for that was all he was now—a stranger.

There had been a time when she would have welcomed him with rapture, but now he roused no feeling in her whatever, not even resentment.

'The family are out,' she told him, 'and I'm alone.' She led the way into the sitting-room. 'I was astounded to see you. Sit down and tell me how you come to be here. I thought you were at the other side of the world.'

Raymond subsided into an armchair and looked about him appreciatively.

'I thought you'd be startled to see me,' he said with satisfaction. 'Nice little pad you've got here, but almost too perfect. May I smoke, or will that desecrate this spotless shrine?'

'So long as you don't sling ash on the floor like you used to do,' she told him, passing him an ashtray.

Raymond felt the need of a cigarette to support him. His welcome had not been as warm as he had expected. Imogen was never one to bear rancour, but he knew he had treated her badly. He had counted upon her being so overjoyed to see him that she would forgive him, but she was changed. There was an aloofness about this pale, still girl in her white jumper and white trousers that was disconcerting, and there was no light in the green eyes that were studying him a little quizzically.

'May I take this off?' he asked. He was wearing a quilted anorak and the centrally heated flat was hot. The heating, like everything else in Sweden, was always efficient.

'Of course, and I'll make you a cup of tea, but first tell me how you come to be here.'

Raymond's black curly hair grew almost to his shoulders, he too was thinner than she remembered him and somehow he had managed to acquire a tan, if it was not faked. He was looking spectacularly handsome, and was well aware of it, she thought.

'I'm in a musical that's playing here for a week, then we go on to Berlin. It's an ultra-modern show, Imo, in which most of us appear practically all bare. I was picked because I strip well.' He looked complacent.

Imogen wrinkled her nose with faint distaste.

'I don't appreciate this modern craze for nudity,' she said. 'Most people look better with their clothes on.'

'Not a picked bunch like we are, and the people here aren't fussy,' he said lightly. 'They discard their garments at every opportunity, and I must say most of 'em have good bodies. But what induced you to come to Sweden?'

Louise had disclosed her whereabouts but had not told him what she was doing.

'That's a long story,' she said, her face clouding. 'I'll tell you all about it when I've got your tea.'

She went into the diminutive kitchen, glad to be alone for a few moments to collect her thoughts. It was ironic that, eagerly expecting Christian, she had been confronted by her erstwhile boy-friend, the last person she had thought of encountering. But he was definitely erstwhile, she thought wryly; his sudden appearance had moved her not at all, she was not even angry. Once he had meant everything to her, but her feeling for him was dead. In a way she was glad to see him, a familiar face among so many strangers, and the bitter resentment that she had felt at his desertion was also dead.

She was not fickle, she told herself anxiously. Raymond belonged to a phase of her life that was over. Since then she had matured, her experience had widened and deepened. She had learned what real love was.

She returned with a tray of tea and cakes and was able to ask lightly:

'What happened to the Australian tour?'

'It never got off the ground. Cancelled at the last moment, but I was lucky to walk straight into this show.'

'Janice had no further use for you?' she asked with a touch of malice.

'She's an old tramp,' he said calmly. 'I never want to see her again. Anyway, she's gone broke, that's why we didn't get to Aussie-land.'

Imogen smiled ruefully. So much heartache and despair, all reduced to nothingness. Six weeks ago she would have rejoiced to hear Raymond deprecate Janice, now she did not care two straws about his relations with other women. Neither did her heart quicken by one extra beat when she met his ardent glance—and it was ardent, she realised with dismay.

'I've been an awful fool, Imo,' he said with false humility. 'But I've come to my senses now. There was never really anyone but you.'

'I'm afraid you've come to your senses, as you put it, much too late,' she told him bitingly.

'You can't have changed in so short a time!' He sounded almost shocked.

'Why not? You did, in an even shorter time.'

Time, she reflected, in terms of weeks and months meant nothing. In happenings and emotional growth, an era separated her from her old life in London.

'But I'm telling you, I didn't really change,' Raymond complained. 'You see, Imo, we'd always been together. I suppose I wanted to—how shall I put it?—gain experience before I settled down. But now I've seen you again, I know you're the only girl for me.'

'How nice!' she exclaimed mockingly. 'But what was I supposed to be doing while you were gaining experience?'

He had the grace to look ashamed.

'You were always so faithful,' he murmured.

'So you thought I'd be waiting to be picked up again,' she suggested, 'and if you hadn't run into me here, goodness knows when that would have been.'

'I told you I looked you up as soon as I could, but of course I thought you would still be at the flat. We had such good times there—you can't have forgotten them.'

'No, I haven't forgotten them, they'll always be a pleasant memory, but all that's over, Ray. We were only boy and girl together, and now I've become adult.'

She sighed and turned her head away. Her feeling for Raymond had been only a girlish infatuation, another man had taught her the meaning of love—a man, not a boy, but having taught her, he had left her.

Raymond caught the look on her face and he flushed angrily.

'You mean there's someone else?' he asked.

She shook her head, while she played with her tea-spoon.

'I'm out of love, Ray. Can't we just be friends?'

Now she had gone beyond his reach, she instantly became more desirable.

'I was hoping for rather more than that,' he told her with a languishing look.

'That's all you've any right to expect,' she retorted, 'and that's generous.'

'But I've explained . . .' He looked bewildered.

'Not very satisfactorily from my point of view,' she interrupted him. 'Have some more tea?'

'No, thank you.' He was childishly petulant. 'I suppose you can't forgive me for taking an engagement which didn't include you, but you know that in our profession one has to take what comes along. Would you want me to starve while I waited for you to recover from that silly complaint?'

'You couldn't wait to find out if I'd recovered.'

'There wasn't time, and you know that if you miss an opportunity, it may never come again. I came back to you as soon as I could.'

When you'd had enough of Janice, she thought contemptuously. She did not believe his excuses were genuine. He had probably called at the flat to discover how she had taken his loss, and upon being told she had gone to Stockholm, he had come, because he had found himself a stranger in a foreign place. Now he was piqued by her indifference.

He rose from his chair and came to her, drawing her up into his arms.

'Imogen!' he besought her plaintively.

She was passive in his hold, even his touch had lost its magic; the physical attraction that had once been so strong no longer existed. This was the final test, even her body rejected him, and she was entirely freed from her childish obsession with him.

He touched her unresponsive lips. 'What's the matter with you?' he asked angrily. 'Have you become a snow maiden?'

Gently she tried to disengage herself.

'It's no use, Ray,' she murmured. 'It's over.'

They neither of them heard the click of the opening door. But a familiar voice drove them apart, and with flaming cheeks Imogen turned to face a hard-faced Christian with ice in his eyes, while his words stung her ears.

'Running true to form, I see. Sorry we've interrupted.'

Then the room became full of people, for Greta and the children were with their uncle.

'I met Christian on the doorstep,' Greta explained, while her quick glance took in the debris of Imogen's tea-party. 'Won't you introduce us to your friend?'

Imogen murmured names in a scarcely audible voice, conscious only of Christian's withering glance. He bowed perfunctorily to Raymond, while Greta shook hands, and Kajsa sketched a curtsey.

'This is Fru Olsson's flat,' she told Raymond, longing for him to go. 'I'm her mother's help.'

Raymond raised his brows. 'Rather a drastic change of occupation,' he drawled, his tone implying that she had come down in the world. 'Imogen used to be my dancing partner,' he went on, looking defiantly at Christian. 'Since I'm in Stockholm, I of course came to look her up.'

'But of course,' Greta echoed. 'So nice for Imogen to meet an old friend. You're welcome, Herr...?' She stopped, as she had not caught the name.

'Oh, call me Ray,' he said casually, 'everyone does. Actually,' his dark eyes were malicious, 'Imo and I are rather more than friends, but I've been away on tour for some weeks. I gather she hasn't lacked consolation in my absence.'

143

He had noted Imogen's confusion and suspected that Christian was the cause of it. His spiteful remark was designed to drive a wedge between her and the other man. One glance at Christian's stony face showed Imogen how well he was succeeding, but she did not know how to defend herself, for it must seem obvious to him that when she had said her affair with Ray was over, she had lied.

Feeling that he was master of the situation, Raymond smiled sunnily.

'I must be off now. I'm due at the theatre. Thank you for the tea.' His eyes were on Greta, for it was her tea. Resuming his anorak, he said casually to Imogen, 'Be seeing you tomorrow, I hope.'

He bowed to the rest of the company in imitation of their manners and again addressed her. 'Come and see me off, darling.'

Dumbly she shook her head, feeling stunned. He gave her a long, lingering glance, and it was Christian who walked to the door with him and showed him out.

Mechanically Imogen collected the tea-things. 'You didn't mind?' she said to Greta.

'That's quite all right,' Greta assured her. 'You're welcome to entertain your friends, only I didn't know you had any here.'

'His coming was a complete surprise.'

'Was it? How nice for you!'

'It wasn't,' Imogen cried vehemently. 'It was disastrous,' and she carried the tray through into the kitchen.

Why, oh, why of all days had Christian chosen today to return? And how could she convince him that she was not two-timing him? Always with him she had been forced into a false position, first with Peter, now with Raymond. That nasty crack of Ray's contained an unpleasant insinuation, implying that Christian had been a diversion because he, himself was unavailable, and it was quite possible that Christian would believe it. Though he had assured her that he had never accepted her presentation of herself as a flirt, his first remark indicated that he had changed his mind. 'Running true to form.' The words continued to bite her.

Reluctantly she returned to the sitting-room, where Christian was playing with the children, and Greta said cheerfully:

'If you'll bath the kids, Imogen, I'll change the rooms. You won't mind sharing with them while Christian's here?'

That was the arrangement which Imogen had anticipated. Greta used her bedroom as a study and it contained all her papers and files, so she could not also accommodate her offspring.

'Please don't bother,' Christian told her, 'I'll not be staying here.'

She turned to him in blank dismay. 'It's no bother, Imogen doesn't mind, and you promised you'd stay with us. Why have you changed your mind?'

He looked at Imogen, giving her the same icy stare with which he had greeted her. She wilted under it, knowing it was on her account he would not stay.

'I don't want to cramp you,' he told his sister. 'I can easily put up at a hotel near by. I can only stay a few days, so it's not worth disorganising you.'

'A few days?' Greta looked blank.

'Yes. I'm entered for the British International Championship at Aviemore with the Olympic team.'

'Are you?' Greta sounded a little tart. 'That's something you'd forgotten to mention.'

Christian looked apologetic. 'Well, actually I've been substituted for someone who has fallen out.'

'But won't you be coming back here?'

'I'm afraid not. As I'll be in Britain, I'll give Letty and Joe a look and then I must make arrangements about leaving for South America.'

The words struck chill on Imogen's heart. He had meant nothing of what he had said to her. That magic night when the Northern Lights had flared had no reality. That his plans were a complete surprise to Greta was obvious, for she looked taken aback.

'The British Skiing Competitions are a new thing, and quite a challenge—soft snow and a bumpy course,' Christian ran on glibly, though it was obvious he knew skiing conditions were of little interest to his audience. 'They've been so successful they look like becoming an annual fixture. I haven't skied in Scotland before.'

'Yes, but ... America! I thought you were going to spend the summer with us,' Greta complained, while Imogen held her breath as she waited for Christian's reply. He had promised to spend the summer with her.

Carefully avoiding looking at her, he said harshly:

'I've decided it's out of the question. I shall have to keep in strict training to win another gold medal.'

If Greta were disappointed, Imogen was devastated. He could not have more plainly indicated that he was running away from her and his rash proposal.

'Oh well, it's your life,' Greta said resignedly.

'Quite so,' he agreed, smiling, putting a brotherly arm across her shoulders. 'I'd get too soft lounging all summer at your hut in the woods where you'll be going for your holidays, though the prospect has its attractions.' There was an odd note in his voice, and he shot Imogen a veiled glance with a sensual glint in his eyes, which made her wilt. The implication was an insult.

'But I must forgo the temptation,' he went on. 'It wouldn't be good for my morale, nor for anyone else's. Now I must go and book in at a hotel, but tomorrow I'll take you and the children out for the day, so Miss Sinclair will be free to entertain her friend.'

Imogen winced at the use of her surname uttered in

that mocking manner, while Greta raised her eyebrows, but the children created a diversion at the mention of an outing. Excitedly they voiced their wishes.

'A steamer trip, please,' Sven cried.

'No, the zoo,' Kajsa urged. 'We've been in a steamer lots of times.'

Greta tried to remonstrate with them, while Christian laughed indulgently.

'We can go by steamer to the zoo,' he told them, 'then you'll both be satisfied.'

Imogen was completely ignored during the general hubbub. The expedition did not concern her, she was to be left behind, denied Christian's companionship, he could not forgive her apparent lapse with Raymond, nor give her a chance to explain. But it could not be only that; his plans were ready made before he saw her, he could not have concocted them in a few moments.

Fearing to betray her chagrin, she went into her own room, the room she would have so gladly surrendered to Christian, if only he would stay. She leaned her head against the cold window pane. There was little to see outside, only another block of flats rising opposite, a warren of small apartments like the one she was in, one above the other, but each containing its human occupants with their quotas of pain and joy.

The sight of Christian, lean and bronzed, had stirred her pulse in a way Raymond had failed to do. With every fibre of her being she longed to run to him, to tell him that Ray meant nothing to her, that he himself was all she wanted. But she could not do so with the family present, and it did not look as if he meant to give her a chance to speak to him alone.

But if he did not, she would make one. She was not going to let him escape so easily. She would at least ascertain if he still wanted her. That sensual glance which he had given her indicated that he did, and the idea of a summer idyll had presented a temptation which he had resisted. It was only the thought of a permanent union from which he shrank. Perhaps she could overcome his reluctance if she again assured him that she was no menace to his skiing—that was, if she could convince him about Raymond.

She would waylay him as he left the flat and force the issue, for if she owed him an explanation, he owed her one also. She was not going to be pushed aside because he had changed his mind concerning her.

Noiselessly she slipped into the tiny hall and eased back the catch on the front door. She crept through it only just in time, for she could hear him saying good-bye to the children.

The Olssons' flat was three floors up and she ran down the numerous flights of stairs, not daring to risk the lift. He might come out with Greta and catch her going into it. Breathless, she arrived in the entrance hall and saw to her relief that it was empty, the janitor had gone for his cup of tea.

Almost immediately the lift came down, the gate opened and Christian emerged. She saw his face was set and stern, and for a moment she quailed. Then summoning up all her courage, she stepped up to him, her heart beating fast.

'Christian!'

He started at the sound of her voice, and stood like a statue of stone, while she gazed at him with eyes full of desperate appeal. Then with an effort, he said coldly:

'What can I do for you, Miss Sinclair?'

'Give me a hearing,' she said, striving to speak calmly. 'I told you about Ray, you know he means nothing to me now.'

If anything his face became even harder.

'Really? You surprise me.'

In memory she was carried back to the night in Lettice's kitchen when he had disbelieved her assertions

148

about Peter, after catching her with him at Riber Castle. Almost she could have laughed. She seemed doomed to be discovered in compromising situations with other men. But afterwards he had believed her; she must make him believe her now.

He went on in the same cold voice:

'I suppose it was too much to expect that you could be constant for more than a fortnight, or was it, as your friend said, that I was merely a makeshift until he came again?'

'How can you say that? Do you think I lied to you? His arrival was completely unexpected. I thought he was in Australia.'

'Indeed?'

She looked at him yearningly. The overcoat he was wearing could not disguise the lithe grace of his body. A stray sunbeam touched his hair with gold, but his blue eyes were still icy.

'Christian, tell me the truth,' she said urgently. 'Isn't Ray just an excuse? Aren't you regretting what you said to me in Jamtland?'

He moved impatiently, turning his head away.

'What makes you think that?'

Hope stirred in her. 'You never wrote,' she began.

'I'd other things to do.'

She had meant to be calm and reasonable, but the recollection of his neglect sent a wave of bitter resentment sweeping over her. She had so passionately longed for a letter.

'Yes,' she cried wrathfully, 'as you told Greta, gold medals are all you care about. When you got back to your skiing you decided even one summer was too much to give up to me. Perhaps you met some other girl, an Olympic Amazon who is also going to the Andes, and thought she'd be good for a little fun without strings. That's what you're afraid of, isn't it, being tied? You accuse me of being inconstant, but you're just as bad. What about Erica?'

He turned towards her, his fists clenched, while a muscle in his cheek was twitching, but he spoke almost humorously.

'The pot calling the kettle black?'

'Is that all you have to say?'

'I've nothing to say, Imogen, and I see no point in prolonging this uncomfortable interview.'

Her anger died away, to be succeeded by a sense of desolation. He no longer cared for her, but then, she recollected, he never had said he loved her. He had desired her, but that was not quite the same thing, now he did not even do that.

Mutely she turned away towards the stairs, she had gained nothing except a confirmation of all her misgivings, to argue further would only increase her hurt.

He took a step towards her, calling her name, but as she stopped and turned round, he drew back. Silently they regarded each other with a long, questing look. Then, with a muttered imprecation, he turned on his heel and strode out of the entrance door.

Imogen walked slowly back up the stairs, not noticing where she was going, while a few scalding tears ran down her cheeks as she mourned for her lost dream.

She slipped quietly into the flat and regaining her own room, hastily wiped her face. Greta called her, it was time she gave the children their bath. She was thankful that Christian's sister knew nothing of what had transpired between them. Pale and composed she went into the sitting-room.

Greta was looking round her small domain with a slightly rueful smile.

'I suppose it is a bit cramped for an outdoor man,' she remarked. 'He can spread himself in a hotel. As you may have gathered, Christian and I are very close, twins usually are, but we don't see eye to eye regarding accommodation.'

'He prefers the farm?' Imogen asked, trying to sound casual. She was not sure that she did not also prefer the big spacious rooms to this little modern box.

'Definitely, but then he doesn't have to do the house-work.' Greta went on to say that the Spanish business had been satisfactorily concluded. Christian's friend had got off with a fine.

'So he didn't wait to telephone but came as fast as he could to give us a surprise.'

Imogen said nothing. Christian had been the one to get a surprise. She wondered vaguely that if he had not found her with Raymond, what other excuse he would have thought up to account for his change of heart. For that he had changed she could not doubt. Now he was only too willing to believe the worst of her.

Unbidden words of his suddenly recurred to her mind. He had told her on their walk back from the Treak Cavern that if she made Peter suffer, he would punish her. Could it be possible that all his subse-quent assertions of her innocence had been a blind and he had worked to that end? 'You'll have me to deal with,' were his exact words, and he had dealt with her, deliberately arousing expectations which he did not intend to fulfil in a spirit of revenge. The thought was so terrible that she gasped and clutched the table for support. Surely Christian could not be so inhuman, so utterly unfair? Yet the explanation fitted his con-duct, though any pain she had unwillingly caused Peter would be forgotten by now, and it could not compare in magnitude with what Christian had done to her.

'What's the matter?' Greta asked. 'Aren't you feeling well?'

Imogen laughed shakily. 'Sorry, I turned giddy for a moment, but it's nothing.'

Greta insisted that she sat down, saying she would attend to her offspring.

'I expect you find our climate a bit trying,' she said. 'But the worst's over now. We shall have a long summer vacation in the forest which will set us all up before we have to face the winter again.'

'That will be lovely.'

Greta went to bath Sven and Kajsa, telling them firmly there would be no bedtime story that night. Fröcken Imogen was too tired.

Imogen felt a little guilty at this evasion of her duties, she was still trying to shake off the welter of wild conjectures which her encounter with Christian had evoked, she was too shaken to think rationally, but she was glad to be spared the usual fairy story. They always ended happily ever afterwards which so rarely happened in real life.

Her eyes fell on her writing case which she had left on the windowsill when Raymond had come in. Mechanically she picked it up and carried it to her room. With so little space, they all had to be meticulously tidy. It still contained her unposted letter to Peter. A good thing Christian had not seen that, she thought, and then ... what did it matter if he had? Ironically he was at last accepting the picture of herself which she had drawn for him, and which he had always declared was untrue, or was that only a further instance of his duplicity? Every action of his had been designed to lull her into a false security until he was ready to strike, and now he had struck, and struck hard. As for imagining he could really care about her, that had been sheer idiocy. More than once she had been warned about him, and she was well aware that he had only one real love, the sport to which he was dedicated.

Greta called to her to come and have a cup of tea, and she rejoined her, hoping she was not going to talk about Christian. There was only one thing which she could do now, and that was put him out of her mind

... and heart.

Greta discussed the arrangements for the morrow. She took it for granted that Imogen would be meeting Raymond, until she suddenly recollected that the girl had called his coming a disaster. Looking at her a little doubtfully, she asked tactfully:

'I gather you've got your own plans for tomorrow?'

For a second Imogen hesitated. If she admitted that she would be alone, Greta would be distressed, she might even suggest that Imogen was included in the party, and that would embarrass Christian. He was not even coming to the flat but had arranged to meet the Olssons outside, so anxious was he not to encounter her. Nor could she bear to contemplate a day spent in his glacial company.

'Yes, thank you,' she said stonily, and Greta looked relieved. No doubt she was looking forward to having her beloved brother to herself.

Christian continued to absent himself from the flat. The day after the outing, from which the children returned, excited and satiated, with a shopping bag full of trophies, Greta was to have dinner with him at his hotel.

Wearing a low black dress and black furs, she looked very distinguished and very Nordic.

'Pity you couldn't come too,' she observed. 'I might have got a baby-sitter if I'd thought of it.'

'That's my job,' Imogen returned. 'I don't do a lot for my generous salary.'

'Oh yes, you do,' Greta protested. 'But I look on you more as a friend than an employee. You've been a great comfort to me.' She gave her a keen glance. 'I thought there was something between you and Christian,' she went on. 'He was very attentive, but he doesn't seem very interested now. I suppose you told him about the other fellow?'

'Yes, I did,' Imogen admitted, but her confession of a boy and girl affair was not what Greta meant. Luckily the family had been so full of their own outing, they had not got round to questioning her about her own doings.

Greta continued to regard her shrewdly with keen blue eyes so like her brother's that Imogen found them disconcerting.

'Always awkward when two flames meet, past and present,' she observed with a laugh. 'Had you really no idea Herr what's-his-name was going to turn up?'

'None whatever.'

'What a thrill for you. I suppose Christian was just a stopgap?'

'Does he think that?'

Greta shrugged her shoulders. 'Does it matter what he thinks? Do him good to realise he's not invincible. Anyway, it can't have gone very deep with him, it never does. Probably he found another diversion in Spain—the friend may have had a sister who needed consoling. That he wouldn't mention, of course, but it would account for his delayed return. There must have been other witnesses available besides himself.'

'Christian is very loyal to his men friends,' Imogen said bitterly, thinking of Peter.

'Yes, he's very much a man's man,' Greta agreed, 'though he likes his bit of fun, like we all do. But he always manages to detach himself before he can get caught.' Imogen winced, he had detached himself from herself very adroitly. 'He'll be a great success with his feminine pupils when he becomes an instructor,' Greta concluded.

'Possibly,' Imogen said drily, recalling with a little stab which memories so often gave her now his methods with herself. 'When is he going away?'

'The day after tomorrow.'

Although she knew she would have no peace until

Christian had gone, Imogen's heart sank to learn that he was leaving so soon.

'He'll be coming in to say goodbye,' Greta informed her, and went off to her dinner.

Next day Imogen dressed herself with care for Christian's farewell visit, though she expected to gain little from it. She abandoned the white outfit which suited her so well, fearing its associations. Instead she put on the green wool frock which she had worn in Derbyshire. She rubbed colour into her pale cheeks and brushed her hair until it shone, the red lights gleaming among the darker strands.

He came in during the afternoon, his vital personality seeming to fill the small flat. His niece and nephew hurled themselves upon him rapturously. Imogen had noticed that he was much more patient with them than their mother was. Christian's fondness for children was something which she always had difficulty in associating with his character.

'Oh, Uncle Chris, why do you have to go away?' Kajsa demanded plaintively.

'Because I've got to find lots and lots of snow,' he told her, taking her on his knee. 'Soon there won't be any here at all.'

'When I'm a big man shall I be a ski-racer?' his nephew asked.

'I hope so.'

'I don't,' Greta said emphatically. 'It's all right for a hobby, but I hope Sven will devote himself to a proper profession and make his way in the world.'

'There spoke the Swedish mother,' Christian laughed. 'Your uncle, my boy, is a terrible warning, not an example.'

'Why doesn't you have a little boy like me?' Sven asked ingenuously.

'Now that's a thought.' Involuntarily his eyes met

Imogen's, where she was sitting a little apart, feeling an outsider. Hastily he looked away. 'But first I must get me a wife.'

'Fröcken Imogen hasn't a husband,' Kajsa pointed out. 'Wouldn't she do?'

Abruptly Christian put her off his knee, while Imogen was stabbed with anguish. He had said, only such a short while ago, that he wanted her to be the mother of his sons.

'Fröcken Imogen isn't interested in marriage,' he said stiffly. 'It would cramp her style.'

The child looked puzzled and he added hastily, 'Who would look after you when Mummy's busy if she left you?'

'We don't want her to go!' Sven exclaimed. He turned to Imogen. 'Promise you won't ever get married.'

'I can promise you that,' Imogen told him.

'Exactly what I inferred,' Christian said with a sneer, as he rose to his feet. It was the only time since their formal greeting that he had spoken to her and that was indirectly. He looked down at his niece's fair head. 'Perhaps I'll bring you a new auntie back from Chile—a brown one. How would you like that?'

'Don't talk nonsense, Christian,' Greta said with asperity. 'She'll tell that to the neighbours and what will they think?'

'Who cares?' he retorted recklessly. 'I must be off now—got my gear to pack. Goodbye, Sis.'

He kissed her, while Imogen wrestled with her despair. He was going, and without a word to her. She wanted to throw herself in his arms, tell him that she did want to marry—himself, that it would be wonderful to have a child like Sven. But she had to face the fact that she was nothing to him and in all probability she would never see him again.

Yet she had a confused impression that during his

dialogue with the children he had been talking to her, though what he wanted to convey she could not imagine, unless it was contempt.

His leavetaking of her was perfunctory. He merely touched her outstretched hand, while he executed the formal bow which was customary in that country. Neither would he meet her appealing eyes, which desperately searched his face for a sign of softening.

She was left standing alone while Greta and the children went with him to the lift. For the second time in her life she felt her heart was broken, only this time the pain was a thousand times worse, for she loved Christian as a woman with the whole strength of her being.

Sven banged the front door behind him as the family re-entered the flat. The sound had a sickening note of finality. Greta came back into the room.

'Well, that's the last of him for a while,' she observed. 'What about a cup of tea?'

Wordlessly Imogen went into the kitchen and started to put out the cups and saucers.

CHAPTER EIGHT

On the thirty-first of May, the schools broke up and most of the city's denizens prepared to spend their three months' summer holiday amid the lakes and forests with which their country was so plentifully endowed.

The Olssons, in common with many other families, had a hut by an inland lake, where they would stay, but unlike other families, there would be no harassed breadwinner coming out from town at weekends to snatch a brief relaxation.

'When we were at the farm, we never went away,' Greta told Imogen, 'but now I'm a free woman, I'm going to take a vacation like everyone else. Christian arranged about the hut when he leased the flat for me.'

April the thirtieth was a gala day, especially for the white-capped students, who had the ordeal of the *studentexamen* behind them. For this they had worked and studied arduously throughout the year and it was the first step along the road of recurring examinations which would mark their careers, for certificates were everything in Sweden, and woe betide the unfortunate who failed in his student exam. His progress was blighted from the start. But such horrors were still on the horizon for Kajsa and Sven, who had not yet begun school, while Greta's certificates were safely in the bag. In the autumn she would start teaching again.

The last day of April went by the formidable name of Valborgsmassoafton, the eve of the Feast of Saint Valborg. She, Imogen discovered, was actually the English St Walpurga, who had given her name to

Walpurgis Night. Her cult had become mixed up with many old pagan rites, for May Day had always been a very special festival. The preceding night had all the sinister trimmings of a Witches' Sabbath, and of all the four of these which occurred during the year, it was the most important.

Greta had arranged to take the children out to one of the villages to witness the May Day celebrations, which were still continued among the rural communities, and were mainly a survival of old nature rites, as they are in most countries, embellished with modern trimmings.

She had sold her husband's big car and bought a smaller newer model, in which she drove with Imogen beside her and the children in the back seat.

The day was chill and they wore their furs. They found a recent snowstorm had covered the countryside with snow, but a huge bonfire had been lighted in the centre of the village, round which the inhabitants and visitors foregathered to sing a song that began: 'How lovely the May sun shines.' Which seeing that the snowflakes continued to fall around them, was hardly appropriate.

'Never mind,' Greta said cheerfully, as they made their way to a hot-dog stall, needing something warm in their interiors, 'it can't last for ever. Next month the snow will have gone entirely.'

As a welcome to spring, the outing had been a bit of a fiasco, but it was all one to Imogen. Since Christian had gone, it was always winter in her heart.

News of him was scanty. He did well at Aviemore, his successes being recorded in the skiing news. That he was deputising for an absent member of the team was true enough, and that he could not have foreseen when he was in Jamtland. Imogen was quite sure that even if he had not repudiated her, he would have left her to fill the gap, and tried to console herself by reflecting that she would have had difficulty in reconciling herself to playing second fiddle to his sports engagements.

He stayed for some while in Derbyshire; Lettice mentioned his visit in her letter. Erica had given up all hope of capturing him and had become engaged to someone else, a proceeding of which Lettice heartily approved. She did not consider Miss Brayshaw was good enough for her beloved stepson!

Peter was going out with the nurse, and all Imogen received in answer to her letter to him was a postcard of Buxton Crescent, but it was a relief to her to learn that she had been superseded.

Then as all vestige of snow disappeared, the days became warmer and the blossom came out, there was no further news of Christian. He had departed for the Andean slopes.

Greta drove out one Sunday to visit the summer hut, where they would soon be installed. It stood at the edge of a lake, surrounded by forest. There was a large living-room with two convertible divans, and a kitchenette. A ladder-like stair led to a loft with a balcony outside it overlooking the big room below, where the children were to sleep. The place was lined with fibre-glass, with a huge window looking out on to a verandah which stood above the lake.

'It's warm enough when the stove is lit,' Greta told Imogen, 'and later on it gets hot enough to bathe in the lake. Yes, it can be very hot.' She had noticed Imogen's disbelieving look. 'Though it's chilly today.'

There were many other so called huts along the lakeside so they would not be isolated, though most of them were still awaiting their summer tenants.

'Are there bears in the wood?' Kajsa asked a little fearfully, gazing at the shadows under the giant firs.

'There are none here,' Greta reassured her, 'they've been driven away, but we may see some deer.'

Imogen felt she could not wait for the promised summer holiday. The lake and the forest enchanted her. Here in a place which held no memories for her, she was sure that she could find peace and healing.

As a foretaste of the joys to come, Greta lit the stove and they made tea in the sitting-room, but they could not open the window, it was too cold.

Kajsa and Sven scrambled up and down the ladder, delighted with their upstairs quarters.

'They won't fall, will they?' Imogen asked a little anxiously, as Sven hung over the balcony.

'They'd better not!' their mother exclaimed. 'But they're all right. You're too easily alarmed, Imogen. I don't believe in mollycoddling children. Let them learn to be independent.'

Knowing the accident figures for children under five, Imogen thought Greta was a little too sanguine. However, Sven came to no harm, and they all ate hungrily the pile of *smörgas* Greta had prepared for them.

At last the great day came when they locked up the flat and set out lightheartedly in bright sunshine for the lake side. Imogen experienced a lift to her spirits, as if she were closing the door upon an unhappy past. Life she thought was repetitious, she had left London to seek sanctuary in Derbyshire and met Christian. Now she was leaving Stockholm to find forgetfulness in the forest. She hoped fervently that she would meet nothing male there; this time she had definitely finished with men.

It seemed that in this respect she would have her wish. Though there were men and boys among the other family parties, Greta seemed to have no desire to link up with them, and the place was so spacious they rarely came into contact with them.

Days passed in sylvan bliss. They bathed in the lake, fished, and were able to eat their catch, roamed the forest and once came upon a newly born fawn crouched in the undergrowth.

'Don't touch it,' Greta warned, 'and keep quite still.'

They watched with bated breath as the small creature rose shakily to its legs. It looked at them without fear, then it staggered away to where its anxious-eyed mother was waiting, her large ears twitching this way and that as she tried to decide if the intruders were dangerous. They made a pretty picture among the gnarled trunks and young green of the birch trees.

'Could I have a little deer for a pet?' Kajsa asked. 'It could sleep in a box in my room.'

'I'm afraid not,' her mother told her. 'You see, it wouldn't stay little, it would grow into a big animal, like its mother.'

Kajsa looked reflectively at the doe and admitted she was over large for a small flat.

They all became tanned a rich mahogany, but of the four of them, the sunburn became Imogen best. Her hair looked redder under the sun's rays, a tint known in paint boxes as burnt sienna, and her eyes appeared greener in contrast.

Greta asked one day:

'What's become of the friend from England? He ought to see you now.' She was looking admiringly at Imogen's straight, slender limbs, so smooth under their sunburn.

'He went back, presumably.' She could not care less.

'Doesn't he write?'

'No. He was only an acquaintance.'

Greta looked at her oddly. For a mere acquaintance Raymond had seemed to be on very familiar terms with her help. Guessing her thought, Imogen coloured but gave no explanation. Raymond had shot his bolt and gone away again, too peeved by her reception to make any effort at reconciliation.

The Wainwrights were to join them in August, and

Imogen viewed the prospect of their arrival with a faint reluctance. Fond of them all as she was, she feared Lettice would talk too much about Christian and threaten her hard-won peace.

Greta was looking forward to their visit.

'It's a long time since Father has seen his grand-children,' she remarked, and Imogen remembered with a slight shock that they *were* Joseph's grandchildren.

'The generations are a bit mixed, aren't they?' Greta went on. 'Letty's pair are actually my two's aunt and uncle.'

'Do you mind at all about that?' Imogen asked diffidently.

'Not in the least. I like Lettice. Not at all the traditional stepmother, is she? She's nearer my age than father's, actually. It was my mother who was responsible for the break-up of that marriage. It's always risky to marry someone of a different nationality.'

Since Greta was so eager for her relatives' arrival, Imogen chid herself for her hyper-sensitivity. She must get used to hearing Christian mentioned, and talk naturally about him herself. Not to want to see Lettice on that account was unkind and absurd. By the time they were due, she had schooled herself so well that she had almost persuaded herself that she was indifferent to Christian.

They were coming by sea to Gothenburg and bringing Christian's car. Imogen remembered that he had said they could borrow it, remembered also when he had mentioned it, and pushed the recollection away resolutely. That night was something she must not allow herself to dwell upon.

'I expect they'll want to do some sightseeing,' Greta said with a sigh. 'A thing I loathe, but one must be hospitable. Perhaps you'd undertake the duties of courier?'

'But I don't know the country like you do,' Imogen

protested.

'You can mug up the guidebook. I never remember who did what and what so-and-so commemorates, so you'll be better at it than I should be.'

The Wainwrights arrived on a perfect midsummer day. They drew up in the little clearing around the hut, and Imogen's heart stood still, then began to beat violently. There was Joseph, in city clothes, looking a little haggard, Lettice, vivacious as usual, the two children, standing on the turf, dubiously eyeing Kajsa and Sven, and lastly there was Christian.

Greta uttered a squeal of joy.

'Christian! I thought you were lost among the Andean snows.'

'I suddenly decided I'd had enough,' he said after he had kissed her. 'So I flew back just in time to join the party. I thought I'd give you another surprise.'

His eyes flickered towards Imogen with a quizzical look as though he expected to find her involved with yet another man.

Greta went on to greet Joseph and Lettice, leaving Imogen face to face with him. Mechanically she put out her hand.

'It's a very great surprise,' she managed to say with an assumption of calm which she did not feel.

He touched her fingers while his eyes raked her from head to foot. In a skimpy green shift, arms, legs and neck bare, she looked like a wood nymph.

'So you've become a dryad,' he said lightly. 'Your tan suits you.'

His eyes were no longer icy, they were much worse, carelessly indifferent. She murmured something and in her turn went to greet the others.

'My word, this place suits you,' Lettice exclaimed. 'You look a different being from the pale waif who came to us last winter, doesn't she, Joe?'

Joseph smiled. 'After all, she had been ill,' he

pointed out, and kissed her warmly.

'I've seen a fawn,' Sven announced, feeling neglected.

'He speaks English!' Teddy exclaimed in surprise.

'Of course he does,' Greta laughed. 'But I bet you can't speak Swedish.'

'I can,' Pam declared. 'I can say *tack*.'

'That's a very good word to know,' Greta told her, for it meant thank you.

They all went towards the Wainwrights' hut, Joseph declaring that he could not wait to get out of his city clothes. Christian was wearing a sweater and slacks and as they went along, he peeled off the sweater, and also his singlet.

'Good to let the air get to one's skin,' he excused himself.

'How you get tan when you been in snow?' Sven asked with interest, looking at his uncle's lean brown body.

'There was also sun, very hot sun,' Christian explained. 'Well, it's nice to be all together.'

Imogen felt suddenly isolated. They were all one family and she was an outsider. She lagged behind, wondering if they would notice her absence if she went back to Greta's hut. She stopped to look at a butterfly which had alighted upon a clump of wild flowers, and became aware that Christian was beside her.

Startled, her eyes met his, and she saw an almost savage gleam in the depths of them, but he spoke to her with a soft mocking drawl:

'What a charming picture, the sylph and the butterfly ... two of a kind ... but why act the maiden all forlorn? Are you so bored with domesticity?'

'Not in the least,' she returned with spirit, 'but this is a family reunion and I don't belong to it.'

'You could have done,' he said unexpectedly.

'Could I? I wonder ...' She turned her gaze towards

the lake. 'I think I misunderstood you.'

'I certainly misunderstood you,' he told her. 'But I'm only a simple man, easily deceived by women's wiles.'

'That you're not,' she said fiercely. 'It's men like you who make women suffer.'

'But you've thrived.' His voice was silky. 'I've never seen you look better. Who is it this time? One of those?' He indicated a mixed group of young people splashing in the lake.

'I don't know any of them,' she told him indifferently.

'You surprise me.' Now he was sneering. 'No man in train when you're looking more bewitching than ever? I will say for you, Imogen, you're not niggardly with your favours, and with so much promising material around you can't make me believe you're entirely devoted to child-minding.'

She clenched her hands and bit back the furious words which rose to her tongue. She was sure that he was deliberately trying to provoke her and she would not give him the satisfaction of knowing that he was succeeding.

Yet there was a curious undercurrent to his words, as if he were trying to convince himself of her flightiness against his better judgment, as if he were exaggerating her conduct to defend himself against her. But why should he wish to do that, unless ... wild hope surged through her ... he did care and was fighting his feeling for her because he thought she might prove to be an obstacle in his career. But she had told him that she would never stand in his way, that she would accept him as a summer husband only, why should he doubt her?

'If you hold me in such contempt,' she said, her voice shaking, 'why did you come? You knew I'd be here.'

'Must I deny myself my family's company because of

you?' he asked. Then turning his head away, he muttered: 'I couldn't help myself.'

Emboldened, she went nearer to him.

'Then can't we be friends?' she asked, laying her hand on his bare arm, and looking appealingly into his face.

She felt him flinch under her hand, and he thrust it off as though it were a noxious insect.

'No, Imogen,' he said hoarsely. 'And don't touch me, or I may do what you won't like.'

'Are you sure of that?' she asked provocatively, for she was longing for his kiss.

'Stop the Delilah act,' he said roughly. 'Tell me, what's happened to that dancing partner of yours? Is he still around, or has he been given the brush off like poor Peter?'

The mention of Peter Lethwaite chilled her. So it *was* on his account that Christian had played her up. She had not wanted to think that he could be so vindictive and vengeful, and all for a boy who was happily wooing another girl. Possibly he did not know about that, but it was ridiculous of him to credit that Peter was still yearning after herself, unless he was making himself believe it to excuse his own conduct.

Licking her dry lips, she said:

'You've never forgiven me for that, have you?'

'Not at all,' he returned coolly. 'Pete's consoled himself very effectively,' (So he did know about the nurse) 'but it was then that I should have been warned instead of persuading myself that I was mistaken about you until your young actor opened my eyes.'

His voice softened, and he looked at her almost kindly.

'You can't help it, can you, Imogen? I shouldn't blame you for being a butterfly, only...' and now his eyes were steel, 'you're not going to add my scalp to your collection.'

'I only want you,' she told him desperately. 'Christian, please will you listen? I want to tell you what really did happen between me and Ray.'

She saw him stiffen and her heart sank.

'I don't want to hear anything about it,' he told her. 'What I saw was enough.'

'It wasn't what you think,' she persisted.

'You mean you're going to try to make me doubt the evidence of my own eyes?' he retorted. 'You can't do it, my sweet.'

'But up in Jamtland...' she began, and he made a quick movement, as if repelling something painful.

'Forgive me for that,' he said gently. 'I made a mistake. I've since realised that if I married you I'd never have a peaceful moment while I was away, wondering what you were up to.'

'Nor I either!' she cried, stung by his lack of trust. 'For all I know there was a girl in Spain and another in Chile!'

She hoped to needle him by this accusation, but he only laughed.

'There were no girls, Imogen, you have a one-track mind,' he observed. 'I had other ... compensations.'

'Skiing?'

'But of course. You know that's the most important thing in my life.'

'Yes,' she said, with her eyes full of bitter reproach, 'I do know. God help your wife when you do marry!'

'Exactly. That is why I've decided to remain a bachelor.'

Silence fell between them after that pronouncement. From the water and the Wainwrights' hut, gay voices and laughter drifted towards them. They were screened from observation by a clump of young birch trees and a tangle of ferns, enclosed in a secret world of green and gold, the quiet of which was only broken by the hum of a bee, seeking a hidden bloom, and the rustle of some small creature in the undergrowth in pursuit of its livelihood.

Imogen leaned against the bole of a tree with closed eyes. Christian had provoked her into disclosing a mean jealousy and humiliated her by forcing her to betray her need of him. She should have spurned him as he had spurned her, she thought drearily, shown an indifference greater than his, but she had failed to do so because he held her heart. She wanted to cry out that if she only saw him for one month out of every twelve, she would be glad to take him on those terms, but it was useless. He persisted in misjudging her and nothing she could say would change his opinion of her.

The man stood motionless, watching her drooping figure with something oddly like compassion in his eyes. Then he gave a sharp sigh and moved towards her.

Imogen felt his approach and her heart began to race. He came right up to her and took her face between his hands, raising it to meet his eyes, but she kept her lids lowered, fearful they might show the love and longing which was consuming her.

Very gently he kissed her lips and withdrew his hands.

'I thought it would be all over by now, or I wouldn't have come.'

Her eyes flew open as she asked breathlessly:

'Isn't it?'

'Apparently not,' he said shortly, but whether he was referring to her or himself, she did not know. 'We shall be here in daily contact for a fortnight,' he went on, 'so we had better call a truce.'

'I'm willing,' she told him tonelessly.

'Good.' He moved away, then turned back to her with a little rueful smile. 'I'm sorry I raised expectations which I couldn't fulfil,' he said apologetically. 'But believe me, you've had a lucky escape. I'm afraid

I lost my head. Blame the moonlight and the Northern Lights.'

'I did.' She was dry.

'Ah!' He looked relieved. 'Then we understand each other, don't we? Won't you come and join the family party?'

'No, thank you. I must go back to our hut, there are things to do.' There was nothing, but she had to get away and be quite alone. She could not face the jolly gathering who were helping to settle the newcomers in their accommodation.

'As you please,' he said indifferently.

He left her then, striding freely along the forest path, the shadows of the leaves dappling his bare back, the sun glinting on his fair head, but he never once looked round. Imogen watched him go with an increasing pain over her heart. He had not understood at all.

Sitting on the verandah, surrounded by the empty, whispering forest, Imogen went over their conversation again and again, seeking to discover a ray of hope, but there was none. He had admitted that he had lost his head when he had proposed and Raymond had provided a convenient excuse to extricate himself from an awkward situation.

But realising that she expected some sort of explanation, which he must give if they were to live in harmony during the holiday, he had offered a clumsy apology, preceded by the vitriolic remarks which had been an endeavour to put her in the wrong, before he tried to justify his own conduct.

Whatever was the result of her deductions, one thing stuck out a mile. Christian had never loved her, and she doubted if he were capable of truly loving any woman.

The days which followed were for Imogen full of

bitter-sweetness, for she was in daily contact with Christian, and he, after having clarified the situation, as it were, treated her with a casual friendliness, neither avoiding her nor seeking her company, though he was at some pains never to be left alone with her.

The Wainwrights hired a small sailing boat, and since all the children, including little Kajsa, could swim, they spent many happy hours on the water. Christian, Joseph and Greta were all proficient in managing a boat, Greta with the competency she displayed in everything which she undertook. Lettice and Imogen went along as crew, though their duties were usually confined to preventing the children from falling overboard, or being hit by the boom. Occasionally Imogen was promoted to manipulating the tiller, an exercise which she enjoyed, delighting in the way the boat responded to its helm. But she never sailed with Christian. He always took Lettice or Greta.

Time glided by in a sequence of golden sunlight and silvery rain, against a background of blue water and green forest.

During the long Northern twilights they would sit on the verandah outside Greta's hut, warmed by a charcoal brazier, and sing songs, which Joseph accompanied upon his mandolin, an instrument he played with some proficiency. He had a warm baritone voice, and after they had sung themselves hoarse in rousing choruses, he would entertain them with sentimental ditties, of which he knew a number in various languages.

On these occasions, Christian always sat as far apart from Imogen as he could, but frequently she saw he was watching her with a curiously questing look, which she could not interpret. She treasured those evenings, for she was near to him, could speak to him upon impersonal matters, while the warm dusk engendered a sense of communion, which she knew was false.

She dared not contemplate the emptiness he would leave behind him when he was gone, for the Wainwrights were only staying for two weeks. After that, strangers would occupy their hut.

Sven and Kajsa were put to bed early in the room above them, and slept soundly undisturbed by the concert, after a long day in the open. Teddy and Pam, much more spoiled, clamoured to be allowed to stay up, declaring that they loved their father's music. Often both would be asleep long before the session ended, and their parents would have to carry them away to bed. Pam liked to curl up beside Imogen and lie with her head against her knees.

They all wore the minimum of clothes, and the newcomers were soon as tanned as everyone else. Christian, who went about bare-torsoed, looked like a hero from a Nibelung Saga, Siegfried or Sigismund, with his fair hair growing over-long waving in the breeze, the proud carriage of his head on his shoulders and his long, supple stride. Greta so like him, with her long hair loose, might well have posed for a Valkyrie.

Though they wore shorts and swimsuits in the water, trousers were more sensible when wandering in the woods, for the undergrowth could be scratchy and harboured insects.

Once, coming through the forest after a solitary stroll, Imogen came upon Christian and Lettice walking ahead of her, Lettice's slight figure in linen slacks and striped tee-shirt looking childish beside her stepson's tall, straight figure. They were unaware of her, and unwilling to intrude upon them, Imogen slipped behind a many-branched fir tree to wait until they were out of sight.

Lettice's voice was clearly audible; she seemed to be remonstrating with her companion, and to Imogen's dismay, they both came to a halt.

'... intend to go on like this?' Lettice was saying. 'You can't be a playboy for ever.'

Christian's gay laughter rang through the woods.

'I shan't. I've decided to settle down. I'm going to invest the remainder of my capital in a farm, which will also be a ski-school, but I'm afraid you won't see much of me, as it will be in Sweden, though you can always come and stay.'

'Then you'll have to get married. A farmer needs a wife.'

'I've already considered that.'

They passed on out of earshot, and a bitter wave washed over the unintentional eavesdropper.

So he had misled her; he was contemplating marriage, with some sturdy Swedish girl, no doubt, who would make a good farmer's wife. His assertion that he would remain a bachelor had only been a blind to delude her. She could imagine him and a girl in some place like Greta's farm in Jamtland, enjoying the intimacy of the long, long winter nights before a blazing fire, and the picture hurt.

That evening, after a spirited rendering of 'John Peel' which made the forest ring, Joseph softly twanged a few chords and began to sing in his mellow voice.

> 'So we'll go no more a-roving
> So late into the night,
> Though the heart be still as loving
> And the moon be still as bright.
> For the sword outwears its sheath
> And the soul wears out the breast ...

On through the whole three verses, concluding with—

> 'Yet we'll go no more a-roving
> By the light of the moon.'

The wistful cadences died away while overhead a pale moon rode in an indigo sky giving point to the song, and the forest murmured and whispered under its light.

Imogen felt the tears ride behind her eyes, and picking up the sleeping Pam, she murmured that she would take her to bed. She hurried away into the welcome shadows, anxious to conceal her emotion from the others. .

She had not gone far before Christian over took her.

'She's too heavy for you,' he explained his presence, and reached to take the child from her.

Imogen's throat was choked with sobs, and she was thankful that he could not see her face. His bare arm brushed hers as she surrendered Pam. Blindly she turned away from him.

'Aren't you coming along to help?' he asked, but she could not speak. She knew he was quite capable of dealing with Pam by himself.

Like a sad little ghost, she flitted away from him, ran up the verandah steps, with a muttered 'Goodnight,' to the others, and sought the dimness of the interior.

She would never rove again with Christian by the light of the moon.

CHAPTER NINE

THERE was a chill breeze blowing over the water, so they had all opted for a picnic within the shelter of the woods. After walking some distance, they came to a clearing which they decided would be a good place to play. Massed pines and birch sheltered them from the wind, and the sun poured down into the open space.

Teddy had insisted upon burdening himself with a large haversack, declaring he was going to collect 'specimens', but of what, he was vague. However, when Imogen organised a game of cowboys and Indians, haversack and specimens were forgotten. In gratitude for her co-operation, she was shot many times by Sheriff Teddy, but although officially dead, she was permitted to partake of the meal which Greta had spread for them.

'She's in the Indian heaven now,' Joseph assured his son, 'where I'm sure there's plenty of *smörgasbrod*.'

She sat with Lettice on a fallen log while the men and children sprawled on the turf, and utter peace enveloped them. Christian lay full length, tickling Pam's neck with a blade of grass, pretending it was an insect. Watching him covertly, Imogen decided this was likely to be the nearest she would come to paradise while she was in Sweden.

She had not considered her future; she supposed she would return with Greta to the Stockholm flat and face another winter. She felt no inclination to take up her old profession, though the position of mother's help held few prospects. Perhaps next spring she would make a move.

All too soon, Greta announced that it was time they

went home, and Imogen shepherded the three smaller children back through the woods, thinking Teddy had gone with his father. Pam stayed a while to play with Sven and Kajsa, and help put the latter to bed, a proceeding which made her feel delightfully grown up. It was not until her father came to fetch her that it was discovered Teddy was missing. Joseph had thought he was with his sister.

Teddy was a venturesome child, and a little scornful of the younger ones. It appeared that he had gone off on his own and become lost.

Leaving Lettice in charge of the babies, Joseph, Greta and Imogen went back to the place in the forest where they had picnicked. Christian, impervious to the cold wind, had gone out alone in the boat.

There was no sign of Teddy in the clearing, and they decided to scatter, each taking a different path. The setting sun poured golden shafts through the trees, but in places where the conifers were grouped, it looked dark and sinister between their trunks. There were several rides between them, and no indication as to which route Teddy had taken.

'Be sure to keep to the path,' Joseph admonished Imogen, as she started along one of them, 'we don't want you lost as well.'

He and Greta parted to pursue different trails.

Imogen set off bravely at a brisk pace, calling at intervals. Only the birds' evensong answered her. The path twisted and turned and became much narrower. After walking for perhaps a mile, she decided that Teddy would not have come so far and she was on a false trail. She turned about to retrace her steps, and came to a halt, her heart beating fast. Standing in the path, barring her way, was a large stag.

She had been told that such beasts were only dangerous in the rutting season, but she was not very clear about when that was, and he looked very formidable, his ears twitching, while he regarded her suspiciously. He was adorned with a magnificent pair of horns.

For a moment of complete silence they stared at each other, then the beast lowered his head and stamped with his forefoot. That was too much for Imogen. She turned off the path into the undergrowth, determined to try and bypass him. She pushed her way through ferns and briars, and the stag 'belled'; the sound frightening her to near panic, she became convinced he was in pursuit.

But there was no sound of a heavy body threshing through the undergrowth, and her fear subsiding, she turned in the direction of the path which she had left, hoping to strike it at a point beyond the stag.

She did come to a path, but she had not gone far along it before she realised that it was a different one from that she had been on before, and it appeared to be taking her the wrong way. She turned about, retracing her steps, and saw with dismay that the sun was sinking behind a bank of cloud, and the forest was darkening. She began to run, calling at intervals. The path twisted uphill, passed a miniature waterfall descending an outcrop of rock. Hot and tired, she paused to dabble her fingers in the icy pool at its foot. She had not seen it before, and she knew that she was completely lost.

There were dark rides on either side of her in which the dusk was gathering, anything might be lurking there. She was not sure about the country's fauna, besides deer—had not someone mentioned bears? Greta had told Kajsa they had all been driven away, but that might only have been to reassure the child, and they must have been driven somewhere. Why not here?

A rustling in the undergrowth started her off again, running full-tilt downhill. A root caught at her feet, and she fell, twisting her ankle. She tried to rise, and a sharp stab of pain brought her down again. Staring wildly through the trees, she saw the gleam of water and was filled with relief. She must have circled in her panic and there was the lake. If only she could get to it!

Tying her handkerchief tightly round her injured ankle—mercifully she did not think it was a break—she hopped, hobbled and crawled until she came to the water's edge, and discovered to her disappointment that it was not the lake at all. It was a reedy woodland mere, with no sign of a habitation.

Despondently she sank down on its grassy shore, looking apprehensively around her. There was nothing she could do except wait until someone found her. She would be missed, but probably not for a long time. Everyone was looking for Teddy.

Nice idiot I've made of myself, she thought wearily, but I don't fancy a night in the open.

The pain from her hurt ankle made her feel faint and she lay back in the grass with closed eyes.

A slight sound brought her back with a start, and she sat up, looking anxiously about her. Teddy was standing by the water's edge with a pannikin in his hand, staring at her with frightened eyes.

'Oh, I thought you really were deaded this time,' he said with relief.

'I'm all right.' She smiled at him reassuringly. 'But what are you doing here? We're all looking for you.'

He came and sat beside her. 'I get tired of being with kids all the time,' he informed her from the vantage point of his lately acquired seven years. 'And I've found a house.'

'A house?' she asked eagerly. 'Who's living there?'

'No one. It's quite empty. I found it the other day. I'm going to live there. I came down to get some water and then, when I've lighted a fire, I'm going to make tea.'

'Do the others know where it is?' She hoped that

178

Pam at least would have revealed her brother's where-abouts.

'They won't remember,' he said confidently. 'It was a long time—two—three days since we found it when we were out with Dad. He wouldn't let us 'splore it, but I meant to come back and spend a night in it. It's super, Imogen, just one room and a loft . . .'

'I'm sure it is,' she interrupted, 'but, Teddy dear, you shouldn't have gone off without a word to anybody. Your mummy and daddy will be very anxious.'

'They've got Pam,' he pointed out unconcernedly, 'and p'raps I'll go back tomorrow and tell them about it.'

'Couldn't you go now?' she urged, for presumably he knew the way. 'I've hurt my leg and I need help.'

He sighed. 'You've spoilt all my plans.'

'I'm very sorry about that, but I was hurt looking for you, so if you hadn't played truant I'd have been all right.'

He fidgeted uncomfortably.

'I didn't think you'd bother,' he said, hanging his head.

'Of course I did. We were afraid something had happened to you.'

'Ladies always worry too much, Christian says,' Teddy announced. 'He says they're a nuisance, and I think he's right.'

He looked so like a miniature of his half-brother as he made this statement that Imogen nearly laughed. Teddy, she thought, was going to take after him, and some day an unfortunate girl would suffer through his arrogant masculinity. A sharp twinge from her ankle brought her back to the present emergency.

'Please go quickly, Teddy,' she begged him.

He looked doubtfully at the shadowed spaces under the trees.

'It's awful dark now, and it's ever so far. There

might be wolves.'

She did not think there were any of those, but his imagination would create them in the shadows, and there were stags.

'But what can I do?' she asked despairingly. 'I can't sit here all night.'

'P'raps you could get to the cottage, it's only a tweeny weeny way,' he said coaxingly. 'I could find you a stick.'

'We'll try,' she decided. At least this derelict place would provide a roof.

Teddy hunted about, and came back with a stout bough. Leaning on it, wincing with pain, while Teddy hauled at one arm, she managed to stand on her sound foot. Supporting her with his shoulder beneath her armpit—he was a sturdy youngster—and using the stick, they staggered along, and eventually gained the cottage. It had been hidden from her by a mass of tall fern and tangled garden plants growing wild, which reached nearly to its roof. It was a tiny, one-roomed building, with a broken window and a door hanging by one hinge, set in an open space, where the grass had grown waist-high. Inside it smelt musty, but the resourceful child had collected a mass of pine boughs and bracken, which he had heaped in one corner. Imogen sank down upon it with a sigh of relief.

'Chris says branches make a comfortable bed,' Teddy told her.

'You don't mean he helped you to engineer this expedition?' she asked sharply. That would have been very thoughtless, but he would know where to look for Teddy.

''Course not,' Teddy said scornfully, dashing her hopes. 'But he tells me lots of stories 'bout pioneers and 'splorers, and what to do when you get stuck.'

There was a rusted iron grate which he had filled with pine cones and bits of wood. Now he struck a match and the flames roared up in a cheerful blaze.

'Now I'll make you some tea. I found this tin and I washed it,' he said proudly.

She watched with amazement, while he set his pannikin on the fire and proceeded to unpack the 'specimen' haversack, realising that his night out had been carefully planned. Nor had he forgotten anything. There were tea-bags, a twist of paper containing sugar, a tin of milk, filched from Lettice's emergency supplies, biscuits, a lump of cheese, a somewhat battered teapot with a broken spout and a glass jar. For crockery he had unearthed a cracked cup and a tin mug which the former tenants had thrown away, along with a backless chair, upon which he seated himself while waiting for the water to boil.

'This is just like the pioneers,' he said happily, 'and we're luckier than Robinson Crusoe, 'cos I found a house already built with things in it. Which will you have? The cup or the mug? The mug's a bit rusty, though I did wash it.'

'Perhaps the glass jar,' she suggested, 'then you can have the cup.' She did not fancy rusty tea.

The water boiled and he carefully poured it on the tea-bag he had placed in the teapot. The tin of milk he pierced with a nail taken from the wall.

Imogen was glad of the impromptu brew, when he brought it to her, though his implements, she feared were far from hygienic. But she declined the cheese and biscuits, rather to her host's relief. The supply was limited.

The fire died down and Teddy looked at her wistfully.

'Could I lie down by you? I'm awful sleepy.'

'Of course, darling, it's your bed I've got.' He came and snuggled up against her like a puppy, and almost immediately was asleep.

Imogen lay still looking at the square of window

through which the moonlight streamed. Teddy had managed to shut the broken door, so nothing could get in, and outside she could hear the night noises of the forest, the sough of the wind in the branches, rustlings in the undergrowth ... rabbits? A fox? She hoped not rats. An owl hooted, a melancholy sound.

Her ankle throbbed painfully and she was scratched and bruised. Teddy was cramping her, as she tried to ease herself on her uncomfortable bed, but she could find no relief. Time crept by; it could not be long before it was light and then she must persuade Teddy to go for help.

In spite of her discomfort, she must have dozed, for a sound of screeching hinges brought her suddenly awake, and she saw to her horror that the door was opening. Someone, or something, was coming in. For a moment she lay in palpitating fear, wondering who or what the intruder could be, and then the beam of a torch shone over her and Christian said:

'Thank God I've found you!'

With a long sigh of relief, she raised herself on her elbow.

'Thank God you have,' she echoed. 'Teddy's asleep.'

'He'd better wake up,' he said gruffly. 'His parents are half off their heads with worry. It was only when Pam said something about an empty cottage that I remembered this place. But why didn't you bring him back when you'd found him?'

He was only a huge shadow in the tiny room, and he sounded grim and a little menacing.

'Please, Christian,' she faltered on the edge of tears, 'don't be cross. I didn't find him, he found me. I've hurt my ankle.'

He uttered a startled oath.

'My darling, I'm not cross, I'm intensely relieved.' He shone the torch on her foot. 'That looks nasty. If only I had a light!'

'I think there's some fuel left by the fireplace.'

'The what? Oh, I see.' Swiftly he rebuilt Teddy's fire.

'There's matches on the shelf,' she directed.

He turned the torch upon the narrow piece of board that served for a chimneypiece, and soon the little room was full of dancing firelight. He came and knelt beside her improvised bed and gently touched her foot.

'Sprain,' he diagnosed, as she winced. 'Needs a cold water compress. I've got a bandage.' He pulled the roll out of his trouser pocket. 'I thought one might be needed. Thank God it's nothing worse.'

'There's water in the pannikin.'

She felt rather than saw his astonishment.

'What's all this? Preparing for a siege?'

'Teddy had. He wants to be a pioneer.'

'He does, does he?' Christian began to wind the wet bandage round her foot and ankle. 'Sorry if I hurt, darling, I can't help it, and this is necessary.'

For the second time he had called her darling, and her heart leaped. She could endure torture to hear him say that. Deftly he bandaged her foot and Teddy stirred beside her.

'Is it morning?' he asked, rubbing his eyes.

'Nearly,' his half-brother told him. 'You've got some explaining to do, my lad.'

Teddy sat up and stared at Christian.

'How you get here?' he demanded.

'On my two feet, upon a clue from your sister. You deserve a thrashing, my boy, and I'm half inclined to give it to you.'

'Mummy and Daddy don't believe in cor ... cor ... something punishment,' Teddy told him.

'They mayn't, but I do.'

At the grim tone, Teddy shrank back against Imogen.

'You won't let him spank me?' he whispered.

'Only cowards hide behind women's skirts,' his half-brother informed him sternly.

Teddy smiled sunnily. 'But Imogen's wearing trousers,' he pointed out triumphantly.

His bandage complete, Christian sat back on his haunches and regarded the couple before him, the pale girl and the impudent child.

Outside the moon had given place to the wan light of dawn, and all the birds were bursting into song, as they started their matutinal chorus.

Imogen put her arm round Teddy. 'Don't be hard on him, Christian,' she pleaded. 'He's been very naughty to run off without telling anybody, but really he's looked after me splendidly, and his resourcefulness is quite extraordinary.'

'I wanted to be a pioneer like you told us,' Teddy explained. 'But I knew Mummy wouldn't let me. Dad might, he understands, but women always fuss so.'

'They do, don't they?' Christian agreed, and now he was laughing. Teddy perked up.

'I made tea,' he said proudly, 'and Imogen drank it.'

'Very brave of her, but where did you get it from?'

Teddy nodded towards the haversack. 'I brought it.'

'Indeed? So this expedition was planned?'

'Of course. Pioneers always plan everything. The only thing I forgot was a tin-opener. I had to use a nail out of the wall.'

'As Imogen says, your resourcefulness is infinite,' Christian observed. 'But now we must be starting back.'

'Oh, must we?'

'Yes. Imogen needs some attention.'

'Well, there was only one biscuit and a scrap of cheese left for breakfast,' Teddy consoled himself. 'Have you had your breakfast, Chris?'

'I don't usually breakfast in the middle of the night.' He stood up and going to the door, pushed it wide open to admit the growing light. 'I think we could make it now.'

'But Imogen can't walk,' Teddy pointed out.

'I shall carry her.'

'Won't she be awful heavy?'

'I don't think so.' He came back and stood over her. 'You can't carry me all that way,' she protested. 'It's ever so far. Hadn't you better go and get help?'

'And leave you here alone?'

'I'll be all right,' she said, though she quailed from the prospect. 'Perhaps Teddy would stay with me.'

'You underestimate me,' he told her gently. 'If the burden is too onerous, we can always rest half-way.' He stooped and swung her into his arms. 'A mere feather-weight!'

'Wouldn't a ... a fireman's lift, I think it's called ... be easier?' she asked as they stepped outside.

'Possibly, but I prefer it this way. It would help if you put your arms round my neck.'

Shyly she obeyed. He was holding her close as a mother holds a baby. Her lifted arms brought her face very close to his. She could see in the pale light that it looked white and strained, and his unshaven cheeks were covered with faint golden down.

The birds had become silent and the dew lay thick on the grass. A little pearly mist was rising from the lake, while a great stillness lay over the waiting earth, a hushed expectancy, prelude to the great moment of the rising of the sun. The air was fresh and cool.

'I must look a wreck,' Imogen sighed.

Christian looked down at her. Her hair was tousled and sprinkled with pieces of dead leaf, her shirt was torn, there were even scratches on her face

'I've seen you look better,' he admitted, 'but never more appealing.'

Teddy was scampering along in front of them, and he bent his head and swiftly kissed her lips.

'Oh, Christian!' she murmured shakily, and hid her face in his neck.

'Oh, Imogen!' he mimicked her. 'Do you still love me?'

'What's that to you?' she asked sadly. 'You don't want my love.'

'But I do. More than anything. Last night was my moment of truth. When I came back from sailing and you couldn't be found, I nearly went crazy, thinking you might be hurt or in danger. I knew then that if anything happened to you, the light would go out for me.'

Joy surged through her, tempered by doubt.

'Do you really mean that?' she asked anxiously.

Teddy came running back. 'Do hurry up,' he urged. 'I'm so hungry!'

'You go on,' Christian suggested. 'You can find your way, can't you? Tell them we're coming, but we may have to stop for a little rest.'

'I thought you'd find her heavy,' Teddy said ungallantly. 'I did, when she leaned on me.'

'There are some burdens we enjoy carrying,' Christian announced.

That was too subtle for Teddy. He looked puzzled.

'She's all scratched,' he said commiseratingly. 'Does it hurt? Mummy's got some ointment that'll make it better.'

'Yes . . . well, go and ask her to get it out.' Christian bade him, and Teddy fled away like a young fawn down the path ahead of them.

He was out of sight when they reached the clearing where they had picnicked on the previous afternoon. Christian sat down on the fallen log, with Imogen on his knees.

Long fingers of light were running up the sky above

the dark trees, heralding the sun. Christian looked at Imogen.

'You *are* all scratched, poor darling,' he said tenderly, 'I wish I'd given that young varmint the hiding he deserved!'

'I'm glad you didn't,' she returned. 'He's a delightful imp, and I don't think he meant to frighten us all.'

'Yes. Let's hope we'll be lucky enough to have one like him.'

This was becoming too like that other night, and sunrise could be as insidious an influence as moonlight.

'You're taking an unfair advantage of my helplessness, Mr Wainwright,' she said crisply. 'Perhaps you could rest better if you put me down, and you should have asked Teddy to send help.'

He laughed softly, his cheek against hers.

'I don't want any help. Do you know what's going to happen to you? You're going to be marooned alone with me on a farm like Greta's—I'm giving up racing —where your only recreation will be learning to ski. Do you think you can bear it?'

'I could bear the North Pole if I'm with you, and I liked Greta's farm,' she said candidly. 'But what I can't bear is your lack of trust. You wouldn't let me tell you about Ray—how he came expecting I would melt into his arms, and I found I was utterly indifferent to him. You've a knack of turning up at the wrong moment and drawing incorrect conclusions.'

Christian's hold tightened.

'I was too hasty,' he admitted, 'but I was mad jealous. I came back to marry you and found you apparently, as you put it, melting in another man's arms. It says a lot for my self-control that I was able to show him out without bashing his face in. I went away meaning to forget you, but I couldn't. I had to come and find out what had happened. Then when I met you again, you were so cold and aloof, I thought that you were hating me for coming, that made me sore. You could have given me a hint as to how the land lay.'

'No, I couldn't. You see, I was convinced that you regretted having proposed to me, and were using Ray as an excuse to get out of it.'

'But, darling, whatever made you think that?'

'Someone told me once that you were apt to lose your head with girls in the moonlight and spent the next day wondering how you could explain that you hadn't meant what you said.'

He smiled a little sheepishly. 'That may be true when I lose my head, but this time I lost my heart as well.' He was silent for a moment while she watched him intently, then he said almost humbly:

'I'm no good at grovelling, Imogen—but can you forgive me?'

She laughed, the idea of Christian grovelling was so ludicrous. Then she raised her face to his and gave him his answer without words.

The sun came up in a burst of glory, drenching the forest with golden light, promising another lovely day.

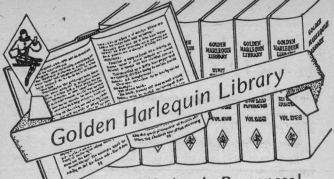

Golden Harlequin Library

A Treasury of Harlequin Romances!

Many of the all time favorite Harlequin Romance Novels have not been available, until now, since the original printing. But on this special introductory offer, they are yours in an exquisitely bound, rich gold hardcover with royal blue imprint. Three complete unabridged novels in each volume. And the cost is so very low you'll be amazed!

Handsome, Hardcover Library Editions at Paperback Prices! ONLY $1.95 each volume. or $11.70 the set

This very special collection of classic Harlequin Romances would be a distinctive addition to your library. And imagine what a delightful gift they'd make for any Harlequin reader!

Volumes 43 to 48 Just Published!
See following page.

x

GOLDEN
HARLEQUIN LIBRARY

20 best sellers

Here are 20 re-issues from the Harlequin Romance Library specially reprinted because of demand.

- [ ] 983 MOON OVER AFRICA
  Pamela Kent
- [ ] 1012 NO OTHER HAVEN
  Kathryn Blair
- [ ] 1021 FOLLY TO BE WISE
  Sara Seale
- [ ] 1024 THE HOUSE OF DISCONTENT
  Esther Wyndham
- [ ] 1031 FLOWERING DESERT
  Elizabeth Hoy
- [ ] 1102 A QUALITY OF MAGIC
  Rose Burghley
- [ ] 1175 MOON OVER MADRID
  Fiona Finlay
- [ ] 1182 GOLDEN APPLE ISLAND
  Jane Arbor
- [ ] 1183 NEVER CALL IT LOVING
  Marjorie Lewty
- [ ] 1184 THE HOUSE OF OLIVER
  Jean S. Macleod

- [ ] 1189 ACCIDENTAL BRIDE
  Susan Barrie
- [ ] 1211 BRIDE OF KYLSAIG
  Iris Danbury
- [ ] 1222 DARK CONFESSOR
  Elinor Davis
- [ ] 1224 SOUTH FROM SOUNION
  Anne Weale
- [ ] 1226 HONEYMOON HOLIDAY
  Elizabeth Hoy
- [ ] 1239 THIS WISH I HAVE
  Amanda Doyle
- [ ] 1244 WHEN LOVE IS BLIND
  Mary Burchell
- [ ] 1246 THE CONSTANT HEART
  Eleanor Farnes
- [ ] 1248 WHERE LOVE IS
  Norrey Ford
- [ ] 1253 DREAM COME TRUE
  Patricia Fenwick

To: HARLEQUIN READER SERVICE, Dept. N 403
M.P.O. Box 707, Niagara Falls, N.Y. 14302
Canadian address: Stratford, Ont., Canada

- [ ] Please send me the free Harlequin Romance Catalogue.
- [ ] Please send me the titles checked.

I enclose $_____ (No C.O.D.'s). All books are 60c each. To help defray postage and handling cost, please add 25c.

Name _____

Address _____

City/Town _____

State/Prov. _____ Zip_____

N 403

Have You Missed Any of These
Harlequin Romances?

All books are 60c. Please use the handy order coupon.

∞